Silver Mo~~

Over 100
Great Novels
of
Erotic Domination

If you like one you will probably like the rest

New Titles Every Month

All titles in print are now available from:

www.adultbookshops.com

If you want to be on our confidential mailing list for our Readers' Club Magazine (with extracts from past and forthcoming titles) write to:

SILVER MOON READER SERVICES

Shadowline Publishing Ltd
No 2 Granary House
Ropery Road
Gainsborough
DN21 2NS
United Kingdom

telephone: 01427 611697
Fax: 01427 611776

NEW AUTHORS WELCOME

Please send submissions to
Silver Moon Books Ltd.
PO Box 5663
Nottingham
NG3 6PJ
or
editor@babash.com

Silver Moon is an imprint of Shadowline Publishing Ltd
First published 2006 Silver Moon Books
ISBN 1-903687-82-9
© 2006 The Authors

Sweet Submissions

Volume 2

By

Kim Knight
Caroline Swift
Sean O'Kane
Richard Garwood
Syra Bond
Falconer Bridges
William Avon

All characters in this book are fictitious, and any resemblance to real persons, living or dead, is purely coincidental.

This is fiction - In real life always practise safe sex!

Sweet Submissions Vol II

Contents

Mia	By Kim Knight;
The Sufferer	By Caroline Swift
Slave	By Sean O'Kane
Pain Ordained	By Richard Garwood
New Orleans	By Syra Bond
The Nun's Chronicle	By Falconer Bridges
Last Resort	By William Avon

Mia

BY KIM KNIGHT

Kim is one of the brightest stars in the Silver Moon firmament! She knows and understands the female submissive psyche as well as understanding girl to girl attraction. A heady combination!

'I can't outrun them in this heap of junk.'

'I told you not to even try,' Mia yelled angrily at the driver, her hand gripping the door handle, 'I've had enough shit from the police. I don't need this!'

'You don't need it?' the driver demanded, glaring sideways at her, 'I've got a bag of fucking smack in my pocket. D'ya think I need it?'

Mia was even more furious, 'You bastard. What are you doing? I asked if you were clean, I told you that I'm trying to stay out of trouble!'

'Well, aren't you just squeaky clean these days?' he snarled, glaring at her again.

'Watch the damn road!' she shouted but it was too late. The car spun, sliding sideways across the road and slamming into a barrier at the side of the country lane. Mia was temporarily stunned and she shook her head to try and clear the lights that were dancing in front of her eyes. A blast of cold are filled the car as the driver's door was thrown open.

'Mickey?' she asked and looked up through the cracked windscreen in time to see him vault the barrier and disappear into the darkness.

'You bastard!' she yelled and undid her seatbelt. She tried to open her door and found it jammed. Cursing angrily, she climbed across to the driver's side in time for a hand to reach in and haul her out of the car. She was pushed back against the rear door and a bright torch shone in her eyes.

'Police officer, don't move.'

She couldn't see the man beyond the light but she knew immediately who it was and her heart sank.

'Well, well, well, if it isn't Mia.' He didn't lower the torch as he spoke but she knew he was smiling nastily, 'Mia – no surname, no fixed abode. Car theft is a bit of a step up from shop lifting, isn't it?'

Mia tried to swallow her fear, 'Oh, come on, Sergeant Kent, you know I wasn't driving.'

'I just pulled you out of the driver's seat.'

'Yeah – I was trying to get out. Didn't you notice that there was a passenger in the front?'

'So, you were the passenger?'

'Spot on.'

'Well then, what a shame that your client didn't hang around to corroborate your story.'

'Client?' Mia sighed angrily, 'I'm not a prostitute, Sergeant Kent.'

'What have we got here?' It was another familiar voice, PC Jameson, Kent's usual partner.

'Either a joy rider or a slapper whose trick has just legged it.'

'I told you, I'm not a prostitute.'

Kent lowered the light to run it down her body, studying her slim lines beneath the battered leather jacket, faded t-shirt and ripped jeans. He gradually moved the light back up until he could see her face and long, straight brown hair. 'Tell that to the whores you hang with.'

'Yeah,' Jameson snarled, 'if it walks like a duck, sounds like a duck and fucks like a duck, what is it?'

Mia shrugged, 'A cat?'

Kent moved fast, slapping her hard across the cheek and knocking her down to one knee. 'Care to answer that again?' he sneered as she lifted herself to her feet.

'What was the question?'

He back-handed her, knocking her to the ground. She lay there for a moment before finding the strength to lift herself to her knees. She looked up at him, 'Is this how you get your rocks off?' The look in his eyes made her instantly regret her words and she hauled herself to her feet, 'Alright, look, just give me a ticket or a summons or wha -' He knocked her down again.

'I prefer you down there.'

She stared up at him. She wanted to move, wanted to stand up and show that she wasn't afraid of him. But she couldn't – she was afraid. She could, and would, stand up to anyone on the streets and had developed a reputation for being someone who would fight to their last breath. But this – this was different. This wasn't street punks looking for an easy bit of cash or a fast fuck – she had no power here and they both knew it. She couldn't fight back and hope to win. Even if she managed to get away, Sergeant Kent would find her and it would be so much worse then. He must have seen the resignation in her eyes because he smiled and it wasn't pleasant.

'That's right,' he announced, 'you know your place.' Slowly, making sure that she was watching his every move, he unzipped his fly. She closed her eyes, turning her head slightly to the side.

'On your knees.' he ordered. She did so, opening her eyes but keeping her head turned to the side. 'Come on then,' he half laughed but there was a tone that made his laugh threatening.

Mia swallowed and then turned to face the half erect cock before her. He was stroking it between his thumb and forefinger and she could see nicotine stains on the edges of his fingers. She grimaced, she couldn't help it. He stank of sweat and cigarettes. He saw her reaction and reached down to grab a handful of her hair, twisting it in his fist and making her gasp as he pulled her head up.

'What's the matter? I'm not good enough for you?' he snarled and then pushed her away. She hit her head against the side of the car and fell sideways. Her hands and feet scrabbled at the road as she tried to get away from him but his foot pushed down on the small of her back and pushed her down, trapping her there. A distinctive sound followed and she knew what was going to happen next. It was Jameson who yanked her arms behind her back and cuffed her wrists. For the barest of moments she dared to hope that they were arresting her and that they would now be off to the station for a night in the cells. But that was too much to hope for. She was picked up and thrown into the back of the car. Kent climbed into the back with her, forcing her to lie down with her head face down in his lap. He held her head down with a hand on the back of her head. He had tucked his cock away but left his flies open and she was forced to suffer the stale sweat smell of his crotch for the entire journey. She didn't know how long they drove for but when she was hauled out of the car she could see that they were on some high waste ground. She could see lights on the motorway below but no houses were in sight.

'That's right,' Kent announced as he saw her looking round, 'it's lovely and quiet up here, no one will disturb us.' He undid her cuffs, 'And, in case you're thinking of playing us up, there's a truck stop a couple of minutes from here and I just know that they'd love you.' Mia stared at him, desperate to see him bluffing but he wasn't. He would take her there and no doubt enjoy the show of a dozen truck drivers having fun with her. Such an image flashed past Mia's mind's eye and she was thankful for the darkness that covered up the flush that crept up her neck. A familiar tingling nestled in the pit of her stomach, she tried to ignore it but it abruptly grew worse when Kent suddenly whirled her around, released the cuffs and said, 'Strip.'

'Sergeant Kent, please, I -'

'Jameson,' he said curtly with a sharp nod.

The constable moved in on her, grabbing the back of her jacket and yanking it down her arms, tossing it away into the shadows. He ripped the t-shirt from her – just shredded the material between his hands and threw it away without even looking where it was going. She was wearing a bra beneath and he struggled with the clasp, pulling her harshly as he struggled to undo it.

Kent held his hand up to stop him and stared at Mia, his eyebrows raised, 'Well?'

Shivering, Mia reached up behind her to undo the bra and slipped it down her arms. Kent held his hand out and she gave it to him. He studied her tight, smooth breasts while he rolled the bra into a ball and then tossed it away.

'If you want to have something to wear when we're finished with you, I suggest that you take your jeans off.' He didn't wait to see if she agreed with him and just walked to the car and leant against it. Jameson joined him and the two policemen lit a cigarette each and then watched while she stripped out of the last of her clothes. When she was standing naked before them, Kent lifted his hand to describe a circle his finger. Taking a deep, shaking breath, she turned full circle so that they could get a good look at her whole body.

'Again.' Kent smiled and sucked on his cigarette. She turned three more times before he told her to stop. 'Not bad,' he commented to Jameson who nodded his agreement.

'Not bad at all for a street whore,' Jameson announced. 'Those truck drivers don't know what they're missing.'

'The night is still young and the slut might still be paying them a visit,' Kent replied as he finished his cigarette and flicked the butt away. 'Come here.'

Mia wanted to turn and run but she had no idea where she was or what was around her. Slowly, reluctantly, she approached the men. She felt patches of grass and dried mud under her feet, she flinched as sharp stones dug into her soles. Once she was standing in front of Kent he lifted both hands to pinch her nipples. She gasped in pain, closing her eyes for an instant and biting her lower lip.

'Don't worry about making a noise,' he told her. 'No one is going to hear you out here. In fact, he pinched her nipples harder, I think I'd like to hear you some more.' He rolled her nipples between his thumb and forefinger, a nasty smile creasing his lips.

'You've got rather large nipples, haven't you?' She didn't answer, keeping her head turned away.

'Hmm,' he smiled again and then let go so that he could open the passenger side door of the police car. He grabbed her shoulder and forced her round to stand on the outside of the door. 'Stay there.' he ordered.

Mia had no idea what he had planned and she watched him as he climbed into the passenger seat and leant over to turn the ignition on. He closed the door with him inside and only when he used the button on the inside of the door to open the electric window did she get an inkling of what he had planned. Jameson had figured it out too and he moved to stand behind her as she took half a step back. 'Truck drivers,' he whispered in her ear as she walked back into him. Kent smiled at his colleague through the open window and then waved her forward. Mia struggled as Jameson grabbed her arms and held her wrists behind her back, pushing her chest towards the open window. Her upper chest pressed against the top of the door and her face was pushed down against the roof as Jameson held her firmly in place, using his body against hers and trapping her wrists in one large hand. She heard the whine of the electric window and her whole body tensed. She heard the two men laugh at her reaction. She closed her eyes and gritted her teeth and then suddenly she felt the edge of the window touching her breasts. She gasped at the coldness of it and tried to struggle as Jameson relaxed his hold slightly so that he could adjust the position of her tits.

'That will do,' she heard Kent say and then she gasped as the window touched her nipples. She felt them being pushed up and then she screamed as the window pinched her hard buds, trapping them against the top of the window frame and squeezing them viciously. Kent laughed from inside the car, tapping the button to gradually move the window up until her nipples were painfully clamped between the glass and window housing. She screamed over and over as the pain lanced along her breasts, tears rolling from her eyes as she tossed her head.

'Please!' she managed to cry between screams. 'Please, stop!'

She felt the car move and then saw Kent's face over the roof of the car, grinning at her from the driver's side. 'Pardon?'

'Please ...' she gasped, '... it hurts.'

Kent snorted, 'It's supposed to.'

'Please ... I'll do anything ...'

He tipped his head slightly to the side, 'Yeah, I know. But you'll do whatever we want anyway, you haven't got a choice in that.'

She stared at him through tear-filled eyes, shaking her head, 'I beg you,' she whispered.

'Pathetic,' he sighed, shaking his head and then disappeared into the car. Mia cried out with relief as the window was opened and then she gasped loudly as the blood flowed back into her misshapen nipples. She leant her cheek against the cool roof of the car and tried to steady her breathing. She was shivering uncontrollably and barely felt Jameson's hands on her sides as he slid her along the car until she was standing in the middle. She looked up as she felt something being tied around her wrist and realised that Kent had found some rope. He was leaning across the roof of the car to tie one end around her right wrist. He pulled it to his side and through the window to loop it through the handle above the door. He then fed the rope through the driver's door and tied it securely around her other wrist before feeding it back through the window and securing it to the steering wheel. He tested the rope, nodding with satisfaction when he found it taut and her arms tightly stretched. The car was cold where her body pressed against it and increased the shivers that ran through her body. She gasped as her ankles were suddenly pulled apart and rope slipped around them. Jameson and Kent worked at the same time to secure her ankles, pulling her legs apart and keeping them wide by looping the rope around the front and back bumpers. The two men then stepped back to admire Mia who was stretched painfully across the side of the car. She was stretched so tightly that the quivers of cold and fear were now little more than ripples running along her skin. She should have known what was to come next but was perhaps too numbed by everything else to fully believe it. Kent had slipped his belt from his trousers and wrapped the buckle end around his wrist. The rest of the length of leather was delivered across the centre of her tight rump with a resounding snap that drew a shocked cry from Mia's lips. Another blow and Mia screamed as fire seared her buttocks. She managed to look over her shoulder in time to see the third blow as it found the backs of her thighs. She screamed over and over as blow after blow fell upon her smooth, virgin buttocks. The belt became like a knife slicing her flesh and at the same time driving hot needles into her skin. But even as her arse and thighs were engulfed in flame, a freezing chill ran up her spine and down her chest. Her nipples though, remained hot and aching, a constant reminder of what the men had already done. It became impossible to tell one blow from another as her bruised buttocks succumbed to the wide belt. When he finally finished she sobbed with relief, only to scream again when his open palm found her buttock with a loud Smack!. Kent moved round to the other side of the car and leant his forearms on the roof, a cigarette hanging out of the side of his mouth as he studied her tear stained face. Suddenly the belt found her buttocks again and she screamed loudly, her eyes pleading with Kent who merely smiled back as his colleague beat her mercilessly. When he finished Mia dared to hope that they were finished with her but then she saw the hungry look in Kent's eyes and she knew that there was more to come. He walked back round the car and she rested her head against the roof, awaiting the inevitable. She felt a smooth dome pushing at her cunt lips and then she couldn't help but gasp as she felt her vagina opened. She gasped again as she felt something cold and smooth sliding into her – she had expected either of the men to slide his cock in but this ... she glanced over her shoulder and Kent slowly withdrew the object, making her gasp. He lifted the glistening truncheon and raised his eyebrows, 'Well, well, well,' he laughed. 'It seems that we have a little pain slut here.'

Mia had heard the term before but to hear it directed at her made her buttocks tighten. She gasped at the resulting ache and turned back to rest her head against the roof of the car again. She almost cried out when she felt the truncheon sliding into her once more, forcing its way deep inside her cunt. She could feel her juices sliding down the polished wood, couldn't stop the pleasurable quivers from running up and down her spine. For a moment she convinced herself that she was dreaming. That this was just one of those strange dreams that she had frequently. Any moment now she would wake up and bury her hand between her legs to ease the painful arousal. It was all a dream … it had to be a dream. She cried out as her pussy clenched around the sliding phallus and then gasped loudly as the ribbed handle pressed against her opening.

'Jesus fucking Christ,' Kent said loudly, his voice half amused and half astounded. 'The little fucking slut has taken the whole thing.'

'That's not possible,' Jameson argued as he moved to look for himself and then laughed. 'Bloody hell. I wonder what else she can take.'

Mia looked over her shoulder, about to beg with the men to let her go, surely they had had their fun, what more could they want from her. Any words died on her lips and her eyes widened when she saw Jameson slip his own truncheon from its holder.

'You ever had anything up your arse?' he asked and then laughed at the terrified look that flashed across her face. 'I guess not then.'

Kent waved his hand, 'Save that for later … I want to see if her pussy can take both of them.'

'Please, don't,' Mia whispered but they ignored her and she was left to shudder with fear as Jameson knelt down beside Kent. She gasped as the truncheon inside her was pulled out a little and then a cry escaped her lips as she felt the second sliding alongside the first.

'Fuck me,' Kent gasped, no humour in his voice now, just complete astonishment, 'keep going, mate, I reckon she's gonna take it.'

Mia screamed as her cunt was stretched painfully and she tried to struggle but the rope held her stretched and she could barely move. The only part that moved freely was her head and she tossed it from side to side, screaming for them to leave her alone.

'That'll do,' Kent announced and then said, 'here, hold mine, I gotta get a picture of this 'cos no one will ever believe me otherwise.' Mia felt hot tears sliding down her cheeks as she closed her eyes against the stinging white flash. Kent took several shots of her spread cunt and then stood beside her to show her the screen on his mobile phone. She stared at the screen, not really believing what she was seeing. He had taken a shot that clearly showed the two wooden shafts sticking out of her pussy but he had also managed to capture the bottom of her buttocks with the harsh welts striped across them. She stared at her bruised buttocks, slowly shaking her head from side to side. He snapped the phone shut, making her jump. 'Right then, let's get you untied.'

Mia almost sobbed with relief as Jameson slipped the truncheons from her pussy and then the two men untied her wrists and ankles. Once she was free she looked around for her clothes but Kent just laughed and pushed her against the car again. 'Stupid slut, you don't really think that we're finished with you yet, do you?' He laughed again and then forced her hands behind her back, trapping her wrists into a pair of handcuffs. He yanked her away from the car and pulled the door open. 'Sit down there,' he ordered and pushed her down onto the back seat, smiling as she cried out at the pain in her buttocks. 'Don't think about going anywhere, we'll be watching.'

Mia shivered uncontrollably as she watched the two men smoking a few feet away. There was no point in contemplating an escape because she doubted that her legs would have the strength to carry her far. She closed her eyes and tried to gather her strength, forcing herself to stop crying. When she opened her eyes she saw Jameson talking on the phone. He said something to Kent who nodded and then both men looked at her before they laughed loudly. Jameson spoke into the phone again and Kent slowly walked over to her, flicking his cigarette away. As he neared he slowly unfastened his trousers. Mia tried to back up, crying out as the seat scratched her battered buttocks. Kent grabbed her ankles and pulled her towards him until her arse was on the edge of the seat. He dropped to his knees and freed his hard cock from his trousers before pushing between her legs. She cried out at the first touch of his cock against her sore pussy and struggled to get away, twisting from side to side. He dug his fingers into her thighs to keep her still as he drove himself forward, burying himself as deep as he could go. He grunted as he thrust back and forth, lowering his mouth to her breast so that he could harshly suck the smooth skin there. She cried out again and then again as he thrust forward, her hips rising up to meet him. He was as surprised by her reaction as she was and smiled down at her.

'You like that?' he asked and thrust down again, crushing her against the car seat. She cried out again but it was more than just a pained reaction. 'Well?' he demanded and thrust again.

'No,' Mia cried out but the uplift of her hips told them both otherwise and he laughed before grunting again and thrusting as hard as he could. Suddenly he gripped her breasts and made her cry out as he drove forward and held himself deep inside her. He held himself there for a moment and then pulled free to tuck himself back into his trousers. He climbed to his feet and turned to Jameson, 'Your turn, mate.'

'Cheers.' Jameson dropped to his knees and gripped Mia's thighs, turning her over so that she was on her front. He slapped her bruised arse a few times and then pushed forward into her semen soaked pussy. He gripped her hips painfully, pulling her back onto his cock as he thrust forward, slapping the backs of her thighs with his own. He was quicker than Kent and pulled free to milk his semen over her welt striped buttocks. Mia was left quivering on the back seat while he tucked himself away.

'Bring her round here,' Kent ordered from the back of the car.

'Alright, just a sec.' Jameson fastened his trousers and then hauled her out of the car, pulling her round to where Kent was standing, looking down at something. Jameson frowned and followed his line of sight before saying, 'You sure?'

'Yeah, why not? The whore just took two cop-sticks up her twat didn't she?'

The younger officer shrugged, 'True.'

'Well, come on then.'

Mia stared in confusion at the two men as they grabbed her arms and pushed her towards the back of the car. They forced her to her knees and then lifted her back until she felt something cold pushing at her slippery cunt. Suddenly she realised what it was and tried to stand up, her thighs straining with the effort but the two men were too strong for her and her pussy was forced onto the ball-like tow hitch. She screamed loudly, as her pussy lips closed around the slimmer base and then she was on her knees and still struggling to stand while the men held her down.

'We can't hold her like this all fucking night,' Jameson complained.

'Get the rope,' Kent suggested and then he held her until he returned with the rope that had tied her hands. Jameson looped the rope around the handcuffs and then tied it tightly to the bar beneath, forcing her to arch backwards as her arms were stretched downwards. 'Nice.' Kent commented as he stood up and then smiled as he knelt down again. He looped the remaining length of rope around her breasts, binding them painfully and then looped it loosely around her neck before tying it off again.

'Very nice,' he smiled and glanced towards the dark road that they had used, 'That will give them a nice sight when they arrive.' He heard Mia gasp and smiled down at her, 'That's right, we've got back-up coming.'

'They won't be here for a little while yet, though,' Jameson commented.

'True,' Kent agreed and frowned thoughtfully, 'what shall we do until then?' He was staring at her breasts as he thought to himself and then a slow smile creased his lips. 'Find me my belt,' he said and Mia flinched at the words, painfully aware of the prominence of her bound breasts – surely he didn't intend to …

'I wish we had some clamps for those nipples,' Jameson said as he handed the belt to Kent.

'We'll remember for next time,' he responded, making Mia quiver. Next time? Surely they wouldn't do this to her again! The thoughts fled from her mind to be replaced by terror as she watched Kent raise the belt over her breasts.

'No, please don't,' she whispered, making Kent pause.

'And what will you do in return?' he asked, resting the belt over his shoulder, 'Come on, I'm a fair man. Offer me a trade. What will you do that's so much better than me whipping those nice, swollen tits of yours?'

Mia licked her lips and then replied, 'I'll suck you.'

Kent raised his eyebrows, 'Go on.'

'The girls I hang with, they've shown me a trick or two. Put your dick in my mouth and I'll make you come – you won't even have to move.'

'That's a tempting offer,' he responded and then suddenly his arm flew down to deliver the whip across the width of her bound breasts. She screamed loudly, tossing her head as her body sank under the blow, pushing the tow hitch deeper inside her. As he lifted the belt for another blow he said, 'I might take you up on that a little later.' He laughed nastily and swiped the belt down again, making her scream loudly. She thought that the belt being laid across her arse was painful but this was far worse. The tight binding of her breasts exaggerated each painful blow to a burning agony that engulfed her whole chest. The tow hitch inside her was hard and cold, her pussy rubbing against it as she sank under each blow. She was sobbing loudly when he finally lowered the belt and stepped back. She looked down and gasped as she saw her lined breasts, swollen even more now. The flesh pushed and swelled around the harsh rope and her nipples were hard and prominent, a tinge of purple surrounding them where the edge of the belt had connected. Her sobs became quieter as she hung her head and lost herself to the helplessness of her situation.

'Here they are.'

Mia looked up in time to get a flash of headlights across her face. She gasped, closing her eyes and turning her head from the glare that remained on her. She heard an engine die and then the sound of four doors opening and closing.

'Very fucking nice.' It was a man's voice and Mia squinted against the glare of the headlights to try and see who had spoken but all she could see was a blur of silhouettes formed by four or five people. As the men separated to move closer and study her, she was able to count five altogether and her heart sank as she saw them staring at her with that same lust-filled stare that Kent and Jameson studied her with.

'Is she sitting on what I think she is?' the same man asked as he drew closer than the others, his fingers playing with the zip on his trousers.

'Sure is,' Kent replied and received a hearty slap on the shoulder from one of the other men. He smiled at him and then turned back to the man who had spoken, 'You look eager for her, Clive, what's the matter, your missus holding out again?'

Clive half glared at Kent, 'Fucking bitch has left me again, aint she? Still, that's her loss.' He lowered the fly on his trousers and released his erect cock. Mia turned away from him, unable to face it.

'My fucking wife used to do that,' he snarled, 'I mean, I ask you, is it too much to ask to have your cock sucked once in a while?' He ran his thick helmet over Mia's cheek, leaving a trail of pre-come across her skin, 'Open your fucking mouth.' Mia wanted to ignore him but that seemed to be the dangerous option and she slowly looked back at him, parting her lips.

His palm slapped her cheek, 'Open your fucking mouth, I said.' She did as she was told, groaning as he slid his cock between her lips, pushing at the inside of her cheek. He slowly pulled free, 'You ever taken a man all the way?' he asked.

Mia swallowed and gave a tiny nod, 'Yes.'

'I mean all the way?'

She nodded again.

'That was probably one of the tricks that her whore friends taught her,' Kent laughed.

'Well, let's see how well they taught her.' Clive smiled and pushed his cock between her lips again. He held onto the sides of her head and pushed himself deeper. She started to gag on him and he held still for a moment while she relaxed. He closed his eyes and pushed on, enjoying the feel of her body's reaction as he slid over the back of her tongue.

'Oh, yeah,' he groaned as he pushed his entire length into her mouth and held her there. She managed to suffer him for several moments before she couldn't take any more and started to struggle as best she could.

'Alright, alright,' he laughed, gripping her hair and slowly withdrawing before plunging back in. He fucked her mouth smoothly, pushing himself deep and then withdrawing.

'She's got a mouth like a pussy,' he laughed and then groaned, gripping her hair again and shooting his come down her throat.

'Clean me up,' he ordered as he pulled his cock free and held it in front of her. She grimaced as she leant forward to lick him clean, the movement causing the bindings to pull across her breasts. When he was clean he stepped back and tucked himself away before accepting a cigarette from Kent and lighting it. Mia was grateful to see that the other newcomers had collected in a group by their car and seemed uninterested in her for the moment – she knew that it wouldn't last but was grateful for the short reprieve. She moved her thighs slightly, trying to ease the aching cramp that had settled in her hips, and gasped loudly as her pussy gripped the metal. Her clitoris seemed to swell and she shifted again, forcing her cunt lips to rub against the cold metal. Her painful breasts and nipples warmed as pleasurable sensations ran along her skin and she closed her eyes, sighing softly. When she opened her eyes again the seven men were watching her with interest and when they saw her looking at them they laughed.

'Harper is going to love her,' Clive announced.

'Yeah, that's a point, where is she?' Kent asked, 'I thought she was coming.'

'She is,' Clive responded, flicking his cigarette butt away, 'she just wanted to stop by her home and pick something up.' Clive glanced over his shoulder at the sound of a car approaching, 'Speak of the devil.'

An unmarked car pulled up alongside the second police car and an attractive woman, dressed in a WPC's uniform, climbed out. She smiled at the men and moved round to the rear of the car. Mia expected the policewoman to retrieve any of a number of torture devices from the boot but she wasn't prepared for the lithe, young woman who was hauled out. The woman was about Mia's age, seventeen or eighteen, and she was gorgeous. Her long blonde hair and startling blue eyes were incredible and for a moment Mia forgot everyone else and where they were. She was dragged back to reality by the sight of the leather straps that stretched around the woman's breasts, throat, stomach and thighs. Metal studs glinted along the lengths of the straps when the woman moved beside Harper as they went round to the front of the car.

'I'm sure you all remember Kelly,' Harper said as the slave fell to her knees beside her, apparently unconcerned by the rough ground under her bare legs. 'And I brought this along for an extra bit of spice.' Mia had no idea what the woman was holding up but all the men recognised it instantly and appeared to be delighted. Kent took it from her and held it up, flicking a switch at the side and smiling as a blue spark shot across the two small points at the top. 'I've had the voltage adjusted slightly,' she added.

'Why?' Kent queried as he handed it back.

'I got sick of my whore passing out every time I used it on her,' she replied and then, as if to demonstrate, she lowered her hand until the end of the tazer hovered over Kelly's breasts. The slave tensed but didn't move as her Mistress flicked the voltage on and the blue spark shot across her nipple. She screamed loudly and fell backwards, sobbing. 'Of course, it still fucking hurts,' Harper laughed.

'That gives me a great idea,' Kent announced and waved for Harper to bring her slave. He approached Mia who tried to shrink away from him but it was a pointless move, given her position. He untied the bonds around her breasts, throat and wrists and then lifted her free of the tow hitch. She cried out as the metal slipped free of her cunt and then again as he pushed her against the side window of the car. She struggled against him when she realised what he had planned for her. 'Someone give me a hand,' he yelled and Jameson wandered over with another of the men.

'Same as before?' Jameson asked as he moved round to the climb in the other side of the car.

'Sort of,' Kent replied as he and the other man held Mia tight against the car. She glanced sideways when she sensed someone next to her. Kelly was leaning against the passenger side door, her breasts pushing against the window. If she had an idea of what was to come it didn't affect her as she stood obediently, her Mistress's hand on her shoulder. Kelly was studying Mia with a look that was a cross between pity and understanding. She was perhaps wondering how Mia had come to be here and Mia couldn't help but wonder the same thing ... about both of them. Thoughts of the slave beside her were forgotten as she felt the glass of the window sliding down. She struggled again but there was no point as, this time, her breasts were pushed through the opening. She felt Jameson's fingers pulling on her nipples and easing her soft flesh through the window. Kent's hand pushed against her back, holding her in place while the window was closed up. Mia grimaced and then cried out as the edge of the glass dug into the underside of her breasts. Her cry turned into a scream and she struggled anew but her efforts only increased her discomfort and she relaxed, sobbing softly.

'Your turn,' Harper announced and reached in front

of Kelly to lift her large breasts through the open window.

'Look at the size of those beauties,' Mia heard Jameson say from inside the car as he closed the window. The slave struggled slightly at the first bite of the window and then cried out as her breasts were squeezed painfully. Once they were both held firmly, their hands were cuffed behind their backs and their legs spread. Mia felt her shin resting across Kelly's calf and she was grateful for it, taking what little comfort she could from that small contact. Kelly glanced at her, a strange look in her eyes. It was a look that was so similar to the one she had seen in the men's eyes that it startled Mia to see it in the slave's expression. It was a look of pure lust and need. She suddenly realised that the slave's need was as great as the men's – she needed them to abuse her and whether she was with Harper willingly or not, she hadn't tried to run away because of that need. It made Mia wonder why she hadn't tried harder to escape. Could she have run? Had the opportunity presented itself and had she ignored it because of some desire to see how far the men would truly go – but also to see how far she would go too? The cuffs at her wrists suddenly felt heavy and the tight squeeze of the window pinning her whipped breasts was suddenly a heat that spread throughout her body, settling at her cunt and flaring like a contraction of warmth. She looked away from the slave, afraid to see a mirror in her eyes. She heard a strange crackle, distant and muffled. She realised what it was a moment before the tazer found her nipple. She screamed loudly, her pain intensified by the crush of her breasts as she struggled from side to side, her bruised flesh sawing between the glass and the window housing. Of everything that they had done to her, this was surely the worst. The spark found her other nipple again and she screamed pitifully. She struggled as before, despite the additional discomfort that it caused her, because it was impossible not to. She heard herself screaming for mercy and the men laughing at her.

'Mind if I have a piece of arse?' someone asked and Mia prayed that the man who had spoken wasn't talking about her.

'Be my guest,' Kent responded, dashing Mia's hopes.

'You sure, you not got anything planned for this one?'

'Not tonight. This one is being thrown back for now,' he replied and she heard him laugh, 'So, no holes barred.'

'Fantastic.'

Suddenly she felt hands pushing at her buttocks and she cried out, struggling again as the tip of a hard cock pressed against her tighter opening. She had never been fucked there before and she tried to tell them, tried to beg them to stop the man.

Kent appeared on the other side of the car and studied her, 'I do believe our little slut is an arse virgin.'

'Really?' the man behind her said, 'Shit, that's gonna hurt.'

'Stick your cock in her cunt,' Harper announced, 'you'll find plenty of lubricant there. That tazer would have made her cream.'

She gasped as the man's thick cock was forced into her pussy and she quivered with pleasure, astounded to feel the truth of the woman's words. The man behind her laughed and thrust into her a few times before pulling free. His fingers delved into her next as he scooped her juice into his fingertips and spread the thick, musky come around her anus. He pushed his finger into her and Mia gasped at the sudden entry into her virgin hole. He curled his finger and Mia quivered, gasping as waves of pleasure coursed through her.

'She likes that,' Harper laughed. 'Did you realise that she was such a submissive?'

Kent shook his head, still standing on the other side of the car, 'Not until after we had beaten her.'

'Has she come yet?'

He shrugged, 'I don't think so.' He glanced at Harper, 'What are you thinking?'

'I was just thinking that we should let Kelly show her a good time.'

'Now?' Kent sounded disappointed.

'Oh no. Kelly hasn't had the tazer on her tits yet.'

If anything was said after that Mia didn't hear it because suddenly the man's cock was pushing at her virgin hole and she screamed loudly. The thick dome of his helmet pushed hard against her resisting arse and she shook her head from side to side. His helmet was forced in and she cried out as her arse closed around the hard rod of his cock. He groaned as he forced himself in, there was a pained tone to his pleasure and his fingers gripped her buttocks as he was squeezed harshly in her tight passage. He held himself there and then suddenly, with a disbelieving cry, he shuddered and came deep inside her.

Kent raised his eyebrows and looked over Mia's shoulder at the man. 'Impressive,' he half laughed, 'she's that tight, eh?'

'Uh, huh,' he grunted in response and pulled free, making Mia cry out again.

'I gotta have a go at that then,' someone said and then two other voices agreed. Mia stared at Kent with pleading eyes, even though she knew it was pointless.

He just stared back at her, tilting his head slightly so that he could see over her shoulder, 'Form an orderly queue.'

Mia gasped and managed to turn to look over her shoulder at the four men who had lined up behind her. 'Please,' she said to the first man who didn't even hear her as he stepped forward and parted her buttocks. Her anus was still open from the man who had just had her, his semen lubricating her tight hole so that the second man's entry was easier but no less painful. She screamed again and then looked sideways as another female cry joined hers. Kelly was sobbing next to her, struggling as Mia had and she knew that the tazer had found the slave's nipples. The sight of the screaming slave beside them was too much for the man who was fucking her arse and her came as quickly as the first. The next man took his time, ploughing her bruised arse carefully, enjoying the strokes into her tight hole. Jameson continued to play intermittently with Kelly's nipples and Mia couldn't help but watch the slave's reactions. Once the third man had come inside her the last man stepped forward and slid easily into her now well-used arse. He tapped on the window and waved for Jameson to use the tazer on Mia who screamed and struggled. He pushed her against the window, using his own body weight to hold her firm while Jameson ran the electricity over her painful nipples. Mia screamed louder than ever before she swooned and her face fell forward onto the roof of the car. She came to a moment later with the man fucking her arse violently, lifting her feet off the floor and causing even more pain to lance through her breasts and bruised buttocks. He suddenly pulled free of her and she felt hot splashes explode across her arse cheeks.

Mia had fallen forward across the roof again and they had left her for a few moments. When Jameson opened the window, she fell backwards but was caught by a strong pair of arms. The world shifted crazily as she was lifted up and pushed onto the roof of the car. Her ankles were grabbed and she was hauled towards Kelly, her legs on either side of the slave's head. She tried to sit up but hands grabbed her shoulders and held her down.

'You know what to do, Kelly,' Harper snapped as Mia was pulled closer to the slave's mouth.

'Yes, Mistress,' she responded. Her voice was smooth and deep and Mia felt her pussy react to her instantly. The first touch of her tongue was almost as electric as the tazer and she gasped loudly as pleasure swamped her in a warm blanket that grew hotter as the slave's tongue explored her pussy. She groaned and gasped, her hips circling as the slave drew her pleasure out like a musician playing an instrument. It was with her tongue buried deep inside Mia's pussy that Jameson put the tazer to her nipples again. The slave's shocked scream filled Mia's cunt and she cried out, her pleasure equalling the slave's pain. The tazer drew scream after scream from the slave but she worked on and soon Mia was panting with pending climax. She expected them to stop the slave at any moment, expecting them to torture her further by denying her pleasure. But they didn't and as her pleasure crested and the most incredible climax broke over her, she almost screamed her thanks to the men who had abused her and let her have some release. She would have thanked them had her pleasure not stolen every ounce of breath that she had, leaving her shuddering and gasping on the roof of the police car.

They left her on the roof while two of the men took it in turns to fuck Kelly. They fucked her cunt mercilessly, making her scream, pant and groan in equal measure. When they had both come, they left her in an agony of arousal while Jameson opened the window and released her marked breasts. The slave was forced onto her back, crying out as the harsh ground dug into her skin. Mia was dragged down from the roof and made to kneel between the slave's legs.

'You have until we have finished out fags to show your thanks to the slave,' Harper told her and then wandered off to join the men.

Kelly was groaning with unspent lust, her lips pulled back in a grimace as she looked desperately at Mia. 'Please,' the slave whispered.

'Silence!' Harper barked, 'Think yourself lucky that I want to see that whore tonguing your filthy pussy. I'll just have to punish you for that later.' Kelly flinched but her eyes stared longingly at Mia, thoughts of her impending punishment seemed to arouse her all the more. Mia slowly lowered her mouth to the slave's cunt. She had never pleasured a woman before and had only been pleasured herself by one, for the first time just a few moments before. She smelt the musky scent of the two men that had had her and licked tentatively at the sticky juice. She thought she would be repulsed by the taste but she wasn't and, if anything, it was intoxicating. She lapped the juice from between and around the slave's cunt lips, cleaning her outside and within her outer lips. When there was none left to clean, she delved her tongue inside. Kelly cried out, bucking her hips up to meet the thrust of her tongue, grinding her pussy onto the tentative organ. She needed more and tried to convey her need without speaking, for fear of the punishment that would follow. Mia understood her need but with her hands still cuffed behind her back there was little that she could do. She pushed her mouth hard against the pussy, forcing her tongue as deep as she could. Then she pulled free and lifted her tongue to the sensitive nub above. She pushed hard, closing her lips around the fleshy button and sucking hard, running her teeth gently around the nub and making Kelly scream. She sucked as hard as she could and then quickly drove her tongue into the cunt beneath. The slave's back arched as her climax bowed her spine. Her scream was more of a sob as she relaxed and rolled sideways to curl into a ball.

Mia sat back on her haunches, she didn't know what to do as she watched the slave shuddering in the aftermath of her climax. She looked up at the group of seven men and one woman who were watching her with interest. There was something animalistic about the way that they watched her – like a pack of predators deciding on the best way to bring down their prey. As Mia stared back at them she realised that she was so very close to the truth. She glanced over her shoulder. The car that had brought her was just a few feet behind her – she could jump in, lock the doors and get away. She didn't know if the keys were still in the ignition and it didn't matter, she knew how to hotwire a car. She took a deep breath, this was going to be her best chance. She turned to look back at the group, to see if they were still staring or how she could cause a distraction. Her sight of the group was obscured by a pair of male legs and she looked up into the angry face of Sergeant Kent. She saw his hand a moment before it struck her cheek and slammed her sideways.

'Tell me that you weren't thinking what I thought you were.'

She looked up at him from her prone position and she wanted to give a sarcastic response but her fear froze her brain, she had nothing to say. Slowly she shook her head and managed to whisper, 'No.'

'Good,' Kent snarled and spat at her before turning away, sneering at Kelly as he passed. Mia wiped his spit from her cheek and stayed where she was, too afraid to move in case she in some way gave him cause to hit her again.

'Time for your punishment,' Harper announced and Mia looked up quickly, sighing with relief as she watched the woman haul her slave up by the hair. She was made to lie between two of the cars and her wrists and ankles were tied to the two vehicles. Mia jumped as the engines were started and then she couldn't help but stare as the two cars carefully edged backwards, tightening the rope and pulling the slave off the ground. Kelly cried out as her body was stretched horizontally, her legs spread. Harper approached her sobbing slave, a truncheon held in both hands. 'Guess where these are going.'

The slave sobbed loudly, shaking her head, 'Mistress, please, I'm sorry, I -' the slave gasped and then cried out as the first truncheon was slid into her cunt and then the second into her arse. Her cries were abruptly cut off by one of the men who moved to kneel by her head. He grabbed her hair, tipping her head back and forcing his cock down her throat. She gagged on his length, her body swaying a foot above the ground.

Harper slipped a multi-stranded whip from the back of her trousers and held it against her shoulder while she watched the man fucking the slave's mouth. 'I'll wait until you've finished before I whip the slut's tits.'

'That's good of you,' the man grunted as he buried himself deeply, making Kelly choke, her breasts heaving as she tried to relax.

Mia was so caught up in the scene being played out before her that she didn't notice Jameson approach her. She gasped loudly as he grabbed her shoulder and forced her up onto her knees. Then her face was pushed down against the ground and he pulled her arse up so that her cunt was presented to his swollen cock. Mia groaned as he fucked her, the sight of the bound slave in front of her an erotic addition to the pleasure that his cock drew from her pussy. She imagined herself tied like that, awaiting the fall of the whip across her breasts and although her gut tightened with fear, her body tightened lower down as well. Jameson grunted as her pussy gripped his cock and he slapped her buttocks with both hands, making her cry out. 'I'm not fucking you for your pleasure.'

Kent looked over, raising his eyebrows, 'If she comes, I'll punish her for it.'

Mia felt her pussy contract at the thought and Jameson grunted again. Kent slowly walked over, studying Mia as he approached.

'I'll take that whip that Harper is holding and start with your tits. Then I'll whip your arse while one of my friends fucks your mouth. Maybe I'll shove a truncheon up your arse while I whip it ... or better yet, two truncheons and one in your cunt.' He knelt down in front of her, gripping her chin to hold her head up, 'And then I'll whip your cunt before I fuck you until you pass out.'

Mia screamed, her eyes closing as her pussy gushed juice down her thighs and the man who was fucking her. He cursed loudly, pulling away from her and glaring at Kent, 'Did you have to fucking do that?'

Kent smiled and nodded as he let Mia's head fall forward, 'I just wanted to see if I could.' He stood up and walked away. Mia sensed him return and she slowly looked up, although she knew what she would see in his hand. Her eyes widened with fear when she saw the multi-stranded whip and he smiled down at her, 'Don't worry, my little slut, I'm not going to do everything I said.' His words were far from comforting and she couldn't help but wonder what he did plan to do. He dragged her to her feet and forced her over to the car that Harper and the slave had arrived in. She was made to lie down with her feet towards the car while he tied some more rope around her ankles. Two of the other men then lifted her up while he tied her ankles securely to the roof rack of the car. Once she was secured, they let her down and she gasped as her shoulders rested on the floor, her head bent at a painful angle. She managed to adjust her position slightly by pushing her elbows under her but Kent kicked her arms away, 'If I wanted you to be comfortable I would have fetched you a cushion.' She looked up at him as he raised the whip and then she screamed, even before the strands had found her exposed cunt. The leather sliced along her pussy lips and inner thighs, forcing a painful shudder to ripple through her body. He lifted the whip and waited for the shudders to ease before he struck her again. Mia was screaming and sobbing openly by the time he had delivered ten blows to her burning cunt. He stopped and she gasped with relief, only to scream again as Clive stepped forward and forced a truncheon into both of her holes. He rolled them between his fingers and then slowly began to move them in and out. Unbelievably, Mia felt her body reacting to the stimulation and she groaned loudly as her holes were fucked. He drew her to the point of climax and then suddenly pulled the wooden phalluses from her, leaving her shuddering with unspent lust. The whip found her cunt again and her tears soaked her hair as she was beaten again. She couldn't count the lashes that befell her pussy, it was one long agony that had her screaming for mercy. When Kent had finished the beating he handed the whip back to Harper and then let Mia down. He pushed her, face down, across the bonnet of the car and pulled her hips back so that he could painfully impale her on his throbbing cock. Mia cried out, throwing her head back. In the windscreen she could see the reflection of Harper as she raised the whip. She couldn't see the slave but she heard her a moment after the wet leather strands found her breasts. Kent fucked her harshly, his fingers digging into her hips and sliding her up and down the cold bonnet. His fucking became more and more painful and when she started to struggle he had her hands tied to the two wing mirrors. He had said that he would fuck her into unconsciousness but he didn't manage it and she gasped as she felt his come filling her. She slumped forward across the bonnet but there was no respite as she felt another man moving into her. The sound of the whip falling across Kelly's breasts and her resulting cries were a constant accompaniment through the fucking.

After the man had finished with her, Mia was aware that the beating had stopped. She felt the car move and then suddenly a pussy was presented to her mouth. Harper leant back against the windscreen and slid her pussy onto Mia's mouth. 'Well?' Mia tentatively licked between the pussy lips but that wasn't enough for the Mistress and she grabbed her hair, pulling her face painfully into her cunt.

'Pete, give this slut some encouragement.' Mia struggled as the meaning of the Mistress' words sank in but there was no escape and she screamed against the pussy before her as the whip found her buttocks.

'Again,' Harper instructed and then gasped as Mia's mouth was forced against her pussy.

'Again,' she spat, 'the stupid whore hasn't got the fucking message yet.' The whip fell across her buttocks again and Mia screamed before she quickly drove her tongue into the musky tasting cunt. Harper cried out and ground her hips forward, 'Ahh, yes! Again, whip the fucking slut ... ahh! Whip her until she makes me fucking come!' Harper continued to spout obscenities, twisting Mia's hair in her fists, until she suddenly screamed loudly and Mia felt her juice gushing into her mouth. She climbed from the bonnet and Mia slowly lifted her head, the breath catching in her throat as she saw the reflection of all the men behind her. It seemed that they all wanted to enjoy her again and Mia had no defence against them. She stared at the reflection as the first of them moved in on her cunt. He slid his cock into her pussy and then pulled free to slam it into her arse. She cried out, flattening herself against the bonnet as she was violently mounted. Kent had wanted to fuck her into unconsciousness and although he had failed once, he was the one fucking her, an hour later when she finally succumbed to the abuse of her arse and pussy that had been continued without pause. The darkness that surrounded her rode on the back of an unbelievable climax and was as great a release.

When she came to, she was alone and the first rays of sun were glinting off her naked body. She moved, as if in a dream, and dressed in the clothes that they had left her. She searched the surrounding area but couldn't find her underwear or t-shirt. She walked slowly down the road. She wanted to be grateful that she had survived the night. They had beaten and abused her but she had remained intact – they hadn't broken her. She was still Mia. Mia. Mia. Mia. She said it over and over again. Perhaps trying to convince herself that she was the same person who they had dragged up here to abuse and enjoy. But she wasn't, was she? She wasn't the same person. In the same way that she couldn't deny that they had changed her, she couldn't ignore the niggling feeling that they hadn't finished with her. Mia wanted to cry but refused herself the luxury. Things had only just started – if she cried now then she would never survive whatever came next. And whatever that was, she wanted it......

Kim is also the author of the extraordinary 'Unchained' series of novels which combine terrific scenes of lesbian sexuality, domination and submission with very fine male dom scenes.
The 'Unchained' series so far:

Dark Surrender

A Slave's Desire

The Chains that Bind

Slave House.

To be published in 2007; The Making of a Mistress.

The Sufferer

(the Lost Chapter from 'The Sufferers')
BY CAROLINE SWIFT

When it comes to female slaves, Caroline wrote the book! In fact she's written a lot of them and all of them feature strong, beautifully described scenes that carry the unmistakable feeling that one is reading fiction based on very real experience!

A while back Silver Moon brought out, among its host of spicy publications, 'The Sufferers', a story relating the fate that befell two young women of heretical belief in the Cevennes during the early eighteenth century. Captured along with others by the royal dragoons despatched by Louis XIV to root out the growing threat of Protestantism in the realm, the girls found themselves spared condemnation to the horrendous Tour de Constance on account of their exceptional beauty. Through negotiation the two prisoners were exceptionally consigned to the Marquis Francis-Etienne for use by his wife, Elodie, Marquise de Vonnange-Lassignac, a wealthy royalist and owner of a batch of submissive slaves. Stripped naked, chained and fitted with flesh rings, Joanne and Martine joined the other captives in the dismal cellars of the Lassignac château to serve as sex-slaves under the whip and instruments of torment employed by the Marquise, her husband, their high-born visitors, as well as the ruthless retainers charged with the incarceration and disciplining of the prisoners.

After months of brutal treatment, the two victims were unpredictably freed by their Camisard comrades engaged in the civil war raging in the Cevennes. Their liberation, as recounted, entailed a fierce vengeance being meted out to the Marquise and her vicious niece, Anthea, at the hands of their own servants, the latter being obliged under the Camisards' swords to inflict the floggings. Both girls, Martine more so than Joanne, had in fact encouraged their rescuers to administer the retaliatory punishments.

When subsequently the girls managed to find their way to freedom in the Calvinist city of Geneva, Martine became a deaconess. Joanne however began to waste away in that dour atmosphere, yearning to return to her beloved Cevennes – and above all to resume her affair, however exacting, with the Marquis Francis-Etienne. She had fallen hopelessly in love with the man and the demands he made on her alluring body. Despite the further perils that should have cautioned her, Joanne decided to risk the folly of travelling back to Lassignac where, she believed, her lover would not only forgive her but also shield her from his wife's and niece's fury over what had occurred on that fateful day, the 20th of June, 1702.

To her dismay, when venturing to the château amid the autumn leaves in the hope of meeting up again with the handsome Francis-Etienne, she learned from a guard on duty beyond the drawbridge that he had been summoned to join the royal court in Paris. Appalled by the news and the absence of that delicious cock she dreamed of servicing again – this time as a bona fide mistress as well as a whipping concubine, imprudently she lingered a while under the battlements, hoping to catch sight of her former companions whom she also truly missed. Alerted by the sentinel, Elodie could hardly believe her good fortune; the slave's sudden, unexpected appearance was providential. A moment later the wretch was seized and dragged into her presence. What was to betide her, despite her pleas for forgiveness, is recounted in this, the 'lost' chapter of the book, a somewhat different account that came to light later in court circles in Paris.

The 'Lost' Script

The Marquise's first idea, once the 'swine of a bitch' was made to kneel before her, consisted in relegating her to one of more inhuman brothels the family owned, catering for the needs of mariners returning from long voyages overseas. Her whorehouses at Nantes or in Bordeaux, which was nearer, specialized in the use of the whip, and at neither port did a sex slave last longer than a few months, if that, under cock, scourge and instruments of torture, thereafter being sold off on the cheap to some outgoing vessel for use of crew members, regrettably deprived of female flesh over extended periods. Moreover, a slave could be flogged, in the case of foul weather, as a sacrifice to appease Neptune's wrath and calm the seas...

The château's tumbrel therefore set out with the valet Coursel assigned to convey the slut to Bordeaux, the man, like Bouchard, Elodie's major-domo, having been duly pardoned for their part in the sufferings inflicted on the Marquise and her niece back in June. The driver was given full right to use en route the slave's body as he wished. Hog-tied, chained and barely covered with sacking, Joanne left Lassignac to cross the Cevennes in the first chill of autumn.

It was a sullen, pouting Anthea some days later who finally persuaded her doting aunt to change her mind. "After all," she had pleaded, "those parpaillot bastards will not descend on us again now that the dragoons are about. And anyway, who knows the bitch has returned? So why send her hence? Have we not refurbished Uncle Francis's private whipping chamber and is it not serving admirably as a torture precinct? Bring the trollop back, now that your husband, who seemed to fancy her, is up in Paris and won't interfere."

On second thoughts, Elodie finally consented. "Very well, treasure. Tell Bouchard from me to send out a rider and have the pernicious reprobate brought back for punishment. We can always sell off what's left of her later after she's spent a week of penitence with us. But, Anthea dear, I have no intention of keeping her here overlong nor of allowing her to be used by the guests. We all know how talkative they can be. And that's too much of a risk, after what happened last June."

Accordingly, a servant – an excellent rider – was despatched with orders for Coursel to return the criminal to Lassignac. Mounted on the absent Marquis's roan, the man caught up with the tumbrel as it was crossing the Lot river, with still three days' journey to cover before handing the cargo over to Elodie's most infamous flogging establishment for seafarers disembarking at Bordeaux.

Terrified, Joanne was slung head down behind the messenger, wrists and ankles roped under the roan's belly for the trek back to the Cevennes. Her sole consolation was that, unlike the valet who had made full use of her three orifices at each halt of the cart, the servant refrained, anxious not to lose time. The same evening, her head and legs spattered with the horse's foam, the half-conscious burden was handed over to a scantily-attired woman she had not encountered during her previous months of captivity. As she was hauled into the courtyard's northern tower, Joanne assumed the new, shapely recruit was probably the replacement for the merciless Marie-Félice, now serving the Marquis in several ways at his courtly Versailles lodgings.

The prisoner, clotted with the residue of Coursel's ejaculations and the steed's sweat, was stripped of her one covering and hastened down the stairwell to the so-called preparation cellar that she recalled only too well. Passing before a couple of booted, leather-strapped guards playing at cards on what appeared to be a punishment slab that her numbed memory could not remember being there before, she thought one of the men seemed familiar, although both were masked; the volume of the fellow's phallus, lolling between the parted thighs, reminded her of a vicious flagellation and sodomy – and the orgasms – she had once enjoyed from someone similar… Neither of the lackeys spared her more than a glance, being more interested for the moment in betting, but a lewd comment on the size of her breasts did raise her spirits. As she left the autumnal sunlight and descended the steps, Joanne caught sight of the walled compound where the morning floggings used to take place to prepare the slave flesh for the weekend guests who were invited to visit the château and make use of its submissive inmates.

"Step lively, whore," ordered the woman, garbed in an open doublet and tight-clinging leggings, cut away to reveal a neat, shaven crotch. "My name is Melanie and I'm charged with priming your hefty body, and that takes time. You will address me as 'Mistress' when, or rather if, you're given the right to speak. In any case, you're to be hooded up but probably not gagged so that you can perform fellatio and tongue cunt. Your first session takes place tonight, after Elodie has dined." Her use of the divine Marquise's first name dumbfounded Joanne, disclosing a self-assurance rare in an assistant slave mistress when referring to her lofty mistress; if she was not cautious, the nude thought, a return to slavery might well threaten. But the harlot seemed unaware of the arrogance she displayed so unperturbedly. "Your ordeal is being confirmed at this moment at table." Then she added: "You will, of course, undergo it stark naked and chained."

A spasm of fear, mingled with the usual excitement, coursed through the returnee as a rope was tightened round her neck, and the steep descent commenced.

On entering the readying chamber, Joanne found the place had hardly changed since the day when Martine and she had been pierced and ringed there, so long ago, it seemed. The overhead cords and ankle hasps in the paving, serving to stretch the muscle and sinew to full tension, were the same as before, as was the long table on which the shaving was done but now was littered with implements, oils and the flesh rings.

"Place that enticing mass of meat and brawn under the ropes, whore, and up with the arms. Part the legs wide – yes, like that but wider still." The slave mistress's orders, compared with those the departed

Marie-Félice used to scream out, were rather invitations than commands, and Melanie seemed surprised at the readiness the slave showed, Joanne having no immediate wish to become acquainted with the knotted scourge swinging from the young woman's loin belt; lashes on a cold, unreceptive body could be dispiriting.

Despite the sludge and slime blemishing the contours, the slave knew the effect her erotic nudity could have on a dominant. Already the nipples had returned to life and tumescence, the belly hollowing between the sharp crescent of the ribcage and the fleecy pubic mound and soon enough the woman would not fail to notice the emergence of the clitoris from its protective sheath and below that, the inevitable ooze of vaginal fluid, merging with what remained of Coursel's sperm, crawling down the drooping labia…

But the swabbing down of the trunk, dorsal area, buttocks and limbs proceeded without comment. Even the freezing water from the pail and the harsh brush gave Joanne pleasure, her cleansed body listing forward as the mistress's fingers scoured out the anus, and then rearwards for the cunt to be freed of what the valet had pumped into it on the aborted journey north. It was only when the oiling began that Melanie commented on the body entrusted to her.

"You certainly have a spectacular bulk of blubber on you, wench – the sort that Elodie seems to fancy, leave alone Mademoiselle Anthea" – she seemed to be wary of the niece – "and Bouchard who revels in flogging a lavishly fleshed female. Since I arrived here, all I've heard from him have been grouses over the 'spindle-shanked starvelings' he's given to thrash, torture and prepare for the guests... although there are one or two whores he says are worth the efforts he expends on blooding them." Quite suddenly, the girl took hold of one of Joanne's breasts in a grip that cut the slave's breath. "But bulges of this sort are sure to please him when it comes to strangling the roots with the iron clamps and using the cane and flesh tongs..."

"Of that I'm quite aware, mistress," the nude muttered, aware that she was risking the knotted whip for speaking without permission. She even added, as her teat was seized and twisted: "I've been here before and I thought you knew it."

"Have you, indeed! Well, that I wasn't told. Then you must be one of the two slaves who escaped after some sort of drama or other. That was before my time and no one seems ready to talk of it. But now I begin to understand some of the remarks made in the banqueting hall where they chew the cud." She paused, looking up and down the length of flesh she was preparing. "Then why, upon my faith, did you return here? I suppose you know or at least can guess what your succulent, sultry body's in for now."

"I had my reasons, mistress, but clearly I was mistaken."

"You certainly were, trollop. But now I have to finish your preparation." Turning to the table to take up a razor, the piercing awl and a collection of slave rings, she added over her shoulder, "I suppose you know you've been condemned to the torture precinct for a week, away from the other inmates..." That Joanne might have guessed but not for a whole week! Her nipples shrank into the delicious unblebbed areoles, her throat tightening. But what she said was factual.

"You don't need to pierce my teats or the rest down below, because I'm already slit. The rings should enter easily enough, mistress."

The woman seemed relieved as she sashayed gracefully back, with Joanne glancing more closely at the new appointee: although she wore neither veil or mask, the breast summits were surrounded with the identical spiked discs Marie-Félice had always worn in the past – and which were not pleasant when she hugged a slave she was working on; the teats, however, although half the size of Joanne's, stood firm and luscious and were tinted purple, as were the labia beneath the pubic bulge, meticulously shaven and bearing a brand mark, possibly from her own earlier spell of servitude. (It was later that evening Joanne was to discover that all of the staff serving Elodie were now devoid of sex hair, a novelty she had already noticed when being penetrated by Coursel during the horrendous journey to the coast. Such seemed to be one of the Marquise's innovations, along with knotted whips, following her husband's departure for Paris.)

Following the expert cleansing within and without, Melanie used the razor, after honing it on a strap, to relieve the slave's body of every trace of hair that had grown since the escape in June. Joanne watched, or rather felt, the shaving, particularly of the pubis, with a certain pleasure but also with disquiet, since it presaged the cunt was to be whipped and tormented. As the growth was removed, she noticed that the slender woman did not wear the customary gloves but leather mittens that left the fingers free, most probably to manipulate an inmate's flesh, especially the nipples and clitoris, more intimately and painfully. A further glance at the hands, as they raked the armpits, disclosed that the back of the mittens gleamed with sharp spikes, similar to those bristling on the jerkin and down the skin-tight breeches. Imagining the girl's backhand blows across the teats, Joanne swore silently to obey the slim mistress unquestioningly, whatever order was pronounced. And there were those lengths of flogging hide grazing the woman's thigh; however much the slave hankered after a good whipping, the knots on the thongs warned her that dumb compliance was advisable – at least until orgasm exploded. But there too she was uncertain of her rights. Culpable of what she had allowed to be imposed on Elodie, she wondered if indeed she would be allowed to spend. The question trembled on the tip of her tongue – and clitoris – but she dared not risk asking Melanie…

The rings slid into the engorged nipples easily enough and were neatly clamped with the crimping pliers. Only the quite unnecessary frictioning of the engorged teats disturbed Joanne, for it threatened to bring her off. But she controlled herself, even when the four labial rings were threaded through and similarly ladened. Thus six of the seven sites were loaded again with the metal circles she had missed so much since having them, at the same time as Martine's, removed in Geneva. They had virtually become for her body natural adjuncts; without them she had felt dispossessed, her climaxes falling short of their usual intensity. Yet it was the reinsertion through the root of the clitoris that threw the slave into disarray. As the woman crouched before the cunt to extend the pinnacle with the tongs, seeking the elusive hole near the base, Joanne let out a sharp cry. At the same time, she heard the slave mistress's remark.

"Parbleu, now that's what I would call a truly lusty frigging stalk! I wager you use constantly, at least when someone's not sucking it or it's being twisted with the tongs. I've never seen one of such a size – it's like a nipple, mon Dieu, like a thumb! I just hope Elodie lets me use the needles on it. I'll bet," she repeated, sinking her nails into the root, "you really punish it when it's erect like this. How many times a night, whore, do you mash it, eh?" The silver slave ring threaded through the soft tissue and clicked.

The hand withdrew, only to be thrust in the slave's maw to be sucked clean, the mouthful of fingers fortunately preventing a reply. Believing the insertions over, Joanne was startled to see an eighth ring gleaming in Melanie's grasp. The slave mistress smiled, watching the dark violet eyes widen as they stared down at the additional annulus approaching the sweating face.

"Now, up with that head," came the coolly efficient command. "This item will put you in a different category from the common dross that lives chained up in the holding cellar yonder – some of whom you probably know if, as you tell me, you were one of them in the past. But you're to be kept apart from the others," – a condition Joanne had expected, being likely to contaminate the cohort with her guilty presence – "and you're going to pass the whole week alone in what I'm told is the new precinct, a chamber where extreme punishment is dealt out to reprobates." (Where the woman had picked up such terms defeated Joanne – maybe from conversations between the Marquise and her guests at high table where this Melanie, probably naked, helped in waiting on the august company, prior to whipping sessions.) "By all accounts, it used to be the Marquis's private sanctuary where he enjoyed certain privileged slaves…"

Joanne felt her heart miss several beats as she recalled the frenzied, ecstatic hours she had spent there with Francis-Etienne – the chains, the whips and, above all, that tireless cock of his filling her three orifices. Indeed, such were the real reasons for her return to Lassignac. What sacrilege to have turned that delicious, distant room, with its oaken beams and lancets giving out over the lush countryside, into a venue of vengeance and torment! As to the former airless dungeon below, seldom did an obstreperous inmate spend more than a night, or possibly two, down there in the depths. But here it seemed, a whole week, being beaten, maltreated and penetrated was normal. To Joanne it amounted to sacrilege. Profanity.

"Since I arrived here last month," the slender – and talkative – beauty went on, "I've only served there once. A fierce redhead who fought the valets had to be brought to heel. It was unbelievably ferocious. Where I worked before, a slave, however unruly, was never treated like that. But here, Dieu seul le sait, what Elodie had Bouchard and the guests inflict on that carrot-haired bitch was beyond description. She must have done something terrible to deserve that – like you." She paused as though expecting a comment from Joanne, who was trying to recall if there had been a redhead among her past colleagues. "Anyway, Elodie had Bouchard brand the troublemaker's breasts with the white-hot iron. I think she was then sold off to some schooner captain or other at Toulon." Again she broke off to pass a hand over Joanne's teats, the other still holding the nose ring. "And let me tell you, if I heard Elodie aright, you're in for something similar. But, considering what I've heard of you, you'll probably enjoy the punishment they've planned. So now let's get this silver trinket through your septum – at least that's what Anthea called it at table. Keep your head still, since I'm not too used to this." One pair of fingers gripped the tip of the nose and raised it as, with the other hand, she aimed the piercing awl precisely. With a sudden thrust, the point traversed the cartilage between the nostrils.

Joanne let out a stifled cry and then felt the ring easing through the septum and being clamped shut. Though the insertion pained her, secretly she was thrilled to have another ring bedecking her body.

"So now you're complete, with an extra mooring. Bouchard will probably stretch you up by that for Anthea to use the horsewhip across those lavish masses of rump meat. If so and if you value your pretty snout, be sure not to lurch about when you're at full reach on your toes. You wouldn't want to rip the ring out, after all the care I've taken with it, now would you? And keep the thighs apart because she likes to lash up into the cunt and hear the metal chiming." Joanne felt the new lustrous circle grazing her upper lip. The pain was agonizing, but strangely there was no trickle of blood, contrary to what she had expected.

"So, let's get you strapped up, whore," Melanie muttered. "After all, there has to be something sturdy to hold you outspread for the bamboo canes, flogging thongs and ... other things." Watching her collect from the same nearby table a number of restraining leathers, each strop fitted with several iron rings, Joanne was taken aback not only by the new slave mistress's slim grace but rather by her composure; from somewhere deep within her entrails arose a yearning to bed the suave woman and see her pass out as she was licked through one orgasm after another. Even her curved back was attractive when she kneeled down to buckle, competently enough, the braided straps of bull's hide round the parted ankles; she plainly enjoyed her work. When it came to encircling the wrists, each arm being released in turn, the cord replaced by similar bands, the naked victim could feel the woman's studded jerkin rasping the ringed teats. The heavy perfume almost caused Joanne to swoon, so pervading was the odour, as the pliers flattened each rivet.

"Of course, you'll be hooded up for your torments," Melanie informed her," but that will be done once you're chained and spigotted in the precinct. Now for the throat strap, trollop."

Expecting the neckband to resemble that which Lassignac had made her endure previously, the sweating penitent recoiled when the collar almost strangled her. "Raise the head, bitch," she was told brusquely. "This is another of Elodie's ideas – or maybe Anthea's. I can't remember but I do know it was donated by one of the nobles after a journey to the Ottoman lands. It prevents the face falling forward when a slave passes out during a breast caning and risks having her head slashed. Even when you're masked, it keeps the skull out of harm's way, and doesn't hamper you when fellating cock or licking a cunt through the mouth slit. Of course, with your head tilted to the rear, you can't see much of what's being done to you…"

Joanne groaned as the upslanting, rigid verge of thick leather forced her head back, leaving her to stare directly at the arched ceiling above. The new fitment was truly perturbing, for even when the macabre, suffocating slave hood, that Lassignac usually employed to mask a slave, was buckled over the head, the victim, in the past, had at least been allowed to observe what was being perpetrated on her flesh.

It was then that she felt a chain being linked loosely to the ankle straps and the wrists crossed over the rear of the collar, to be clipped to a solid ring set in the leather bondage; such bondage, Joanne knew, was customary at the château when slaves were being shifted from one place to another – for instance, from the holding cellar to the outside yard for the morning floggings or for labour in the fields – and allowed the body to be heavily lashed to hasten its progress. (A stumble or fall, she recalled, earned thirty larrups, delivered over the breasts there and then or alternatively added to the routine morning thrashings.)

"Now you're arrayed according to the new house rules of chattel slavery, we can descend to the punishment precinct," the slender one announced, seeming pleased with her labours. Supposing she was to be led down by a lead fixed to the atrocious neckband, Joanne swallowed hard what she had of saliva when a plaited dog-leash was hooked to the nipple rings. At the slave mistress's first wrench on the tether, the teats joined and lengthened in grotesque pain – but at the same time provided the submissive with a familiar erotic thrill she had almost forgotten since her escape. Little pleased her more than being treated as what she was – a helpless, naked victim of her own innermost desires. Pensively and already leaking down her thigh tendons, she wondered if what was about to befall her did not constitute the true reason for her return to the château. All the same, the Marquis's unforeseen absence did continue to distress her mightily.

The humiliating transfer, by the glimmer of a guttering lanthorn Melodie had taken up in her free hand, then commenced. Joanne used what she supposed would be her body's last moments of composure, prior to the inevitable flagellations, to murmur a breathless prayer. The thought of confronting the Marquise, her niece and Bouchard gathered in avenging alliance almost made her forget the sacred words.

*

At each bend in the upward stairway, Melanie looked back to ensure her charge was keeping up and not risking unnecessary damage to the teats. At the same time, Joanne wondered whether the new recruit wielded the knotted scourge as ferociously as the venomous, departed python, Marie-Félice, used to do. In any event, as the major-domo's assistant – and probably his current concubine, she would not have ascended to that rank without demonstrating her talent when horse-whipping a female body. A further furtive glance allowed the slave to take stock again of the woman's slender build and long gaitered legs; unless the regulations governing the use of slave flesh at the château had changed, the chance of licking that neatly shaved cunt might be possible. She tried to imagine what this Melanie's vaginal mucus would taste like…

As to the savage Anthea, the further a Lassignac slave kept from her and her six-thong, the longer would the inmate survive. Memories of the niece striding into the holding cellar reminded Joanne how the staunchest captives used to blanch, their breasts turning into petrified slabs of frozen meat... The week's victim preferred to concentrate on the worn steps she was negotiating rather than picture Anthea gracing the renovated precinct that lay ahead.

To safeguard her nipples, Joanne had to quicken her tread up the stairwell that the neck flange prevented her seeing clearly. Moreover, the process of preparation, ringing and oiling had lasted such an unconscionable time that it had sapped some of her energy; even the prospect of the whippings to come, of which she had been starved for nearly three months, hardly encouraged her to keep up with Melanie. A brisk jerk on the leash, however, hastened her on. "Falter once more, shiftless trollop," – the woman's voice hissed under the mildewed vaulting, her features suddenly hardening, as the service thong was released from the belt – "and I'll flay your rump. I haven't all day to get you strung up in yon precinct, laggard! Elodie must have finished dining by now and she detests being kept waiting by an idling bitch of a whore." The change in the slave mistress truly unnerved the faltering submissive.

Striving desperately for the next stair, the upturned eyes fixed anxiously for guidance on the arched stonework above, the nude body suddenly doubled up as the lash embedded its knotted length into the rear of the thighs. The blow was followed by two further, full-blooded strokes across the shuddering buttocks.

Joanne stifled a cry, catching her breath as she felt the loads of arse meat blossom into purple ridges. Vexingly, the scourge traversed the fading welts fomented by Coursel when he had tied her to the wagon wheel on the recent journey north. Blindly, the slave felt for the remaining steps ahead.

Halting the sweating corpulence before a doorway arrayed with iron brackets and rows of studs, the lissom one tempered her fury. "Now, on your knees, strumpet, thighs fully parted and let's have that pair of hulking breasts bulging well out. That's the posture you ought to know if, as you claim, you've been here before." Taking up the slack of the lead as her victim fell to her knees, the woman jabbed the whip haft into each breast in turn, crushing both teat and ring deep into the soft lymph. "And keep these beefy knobs you have for nipples fully erect, so that the rings hang clear." The slave winced and groaned as the lead was ripped out of the metal insertions but adopted the prescribed position. "You will wait here," she was ordered, "stock-still, till you're given permission to enter your week's residence of penance." To Joanne it seemed as though the woman – resembling now a menacing witch rather than the attractive slave handler she had appeared to be – truly enjoyed humiliating her, reducing the sufferer to the level of an animal about to be butchered.

Buttocks swaying, Melanie heaved the bossed portal ajar and, lanthorn in hand, entered the chamber. Sensing a waft of torrid air emerge from within, the slave was left alone, trembling in the dark.

Well over half an hour later, it was not Melanie but another female who finally came out to take charge of the kneeling figure; the light from the doorway seemed sufficient for the well-fleshed woman to look the slave over and, to Joanne's perturbation, hook a chain to the clit ring. "On your feet, slut," the order resounded hoarsely under the vaulting, "and follow me." Taking hold of the links, what appeared to the returnee to be also a newcomer to the staff led the naked body into the chamber where earlier in the year Joanne had lost her heart to the handsome and, in more senses than one, ravishing Marquis de Lassignac.

Considerably more solidly built than either Melanie or Marie-Félice, now luckily absent, the woman wore a veil of dark gauze over her face, scarlet-dyed gauntlets and high boots but otherwise was naked. If not a subordinate assistant to Bouchard, she had to be fairly junior in the hierarchy, for she had no scourge attached to the loin belt nor were the areoles encompassed with metal spikes. Hence she ranked low but was hardly congenial as she accused Joanne of being late.

"At long last," she complained, giving the clit a harrowing jerk. "You've certainly taken your time to present yourself, slag, but luckily the Marquise had not arrived as yet. It is I, along with the valet Deljoux, whom anon you'll get to know, or at least his cock, who'll act as your direct supervisors during your confinement here in the precinct. And apparently you are already acquainted with the place, no?" Such at least was what Joanne understood her to say, feeling more apprehensive than in the past when a mere servant had the insolence of addressing her so. She saw no point in agreeing, since Melanie had already mentioned the changes made to the chamber. What difference could it make whether she knew it or not? Again, silence was clearly the best policy.

"Deljoux and I," the slattern went on, "are in charge of the chamber's equipment and appliances. You will address me as Mademoiselle Sandrine but that's by the way, as from now on you'll not be able to speak, since I'm about to mask and, possibly, gag you. Have you anything to say, whore slut, before being put to the whip, instruments, cock and studded dildos?" Had Bouchard been present, her presumptuous air and itemized litany, Joanne felt, could in the past have earned her a cautionary flogging, relieved of those ostentatious boots and veil. But maybe she frequented Elodie's bed, thereby being exempt from reprimand.

Although far from clear, her Breton French riled Joanne, who answered briefly. "As a tutored sex slave and of the Faith, I do not converse with Jezebels of your variety." It was daring perhaps, but well worth the risk. The remark was met by a stony silence, indicating possibly the wench was out of her depth.

By way of reply, the fleshy Sandrine wrenched on the chain and dragged the victim into the room where, in those early summer days, Joanne had become enamoured of Francis-Etienne, Marquis de Vonnange-Lassignac – he who now served in the dazzling splendour of the royal court, far, far away...

*

How significantly indeed had the formerly sparse-furnished chamber changed! In the flickering glow of several candles – the sort that Bouchard had only too often doused in her vagìna – Joanne found the place somehow reduced to half its former dimensions; the space was crowded with threatening structures, bolted or sunk into the paving. Even the window lancets had been walled up, a threatening brazier smouldering beneath a canopied chimney. Quite evidently, meticulously planned pain, probably precluding any trace of pleasure, awaited her; for if the familiar suspension chains were still there, dangling from the upper beams, the new posts, wooden benches, a nail-infested crucifix and the racks of whips and implements were certainly not sweet-smelling beds of roses nor ornaments... All resemblance to the simple room where the Marquis had provided himself and her with such pleasure in camera, had vanished; the place had become a dungeon of duress, a candlelit tenement of torture. Lugged brusquely towards the chains, Joanne felt sorry for herself and a little sick at heart.

As the wrists were freed from the nape, the valet's remarks and Sandrine's retorts regarding the wealth of meat the slave's breasts and buttocks displayed, deeply distressed her; never had the Marquis uttered a single disparaging remark concerning her body, not even on the length of her ringed labial lappets, items he liked to elongate still further with metal weights, before whipping and ploughing into the cunt.

The position Joanne was made to take up hardly differed from that Melanie had used for readying the body – except that the leather, rather than rope, limb bondage allowed the stark-naked length of flesh and muscle to be stretched to its utmost reach, the arms taut above, the thighs wrenched apart in their sockets for the legs to be chained to iron hasps in the straw-strewn flagstones. Never before had the spread of the lower limbs and traction on the biceps scared her so, as she silently implored her shoulder and hip joints not to fail her by dislocating. With a week of penance ahead, they, like the rest of her frame, had a long way to go.

Then came what Joanne had always disliked but to which finally she had reconciled herself: the sedulous Deljoux, evidently relishing his work (probably following a night session, wherever it took place and if he was on duty, when he was allowed to drag a slave to his quarters and add to the damage by using her as he wished), approached Joanne. After tinkering with the flesh rings and wrenching them outward to uncover the vagina, glittering with downflow, he passed the chains over the groins and round the summit of the thighs, joining each linkage firmly below the perineum. This and his following duty were carried out under the fastidious supervision of Melanie, who had made her reappearance, now veiled and doffed of her jacket, in order to emphasize the latent power of her torso.

"Make speed, man," she urged, "the others will be here shortly. The slave must be ready to hear the verdict and sentence. And you, woman," – this to Sandrine – "see to it the bitch's hooded up tight."

To Joanne's dismay, being familiar with the sound from times past, the valet could be heard cranking down, from a hinge on the rear wall behind the sweating nude, the thick length of the ribbed dildo. While the leather helmet was being strapped over the slave's head by the burly female assistant, the slave felt the leather-sheathed knob of the impalement shaft parting her buttocks as it descended down the cleavage to nuzzle into the anal sphincter. With a further adjustment of the rod, the valet eased the greased, lifelike phallic dome into the rectum that fortunately had been slackened through incessant use by cocks, dildos and whip handles. The smooth entry prompted him to comment approvingly.

"This wench has some hole! Hollow as hell. Could take a cannon barrel, mon Dieu! It's like a…"

"Shut your maw, fellow," the slave mistress warned him, "unless you want the same up yours."

Joanne gasped behind the already clammy hood as she sank back onto the shaft, her lower belly bulging, as though pregnant, anticipating the effect on her inner dividing membrane when a second shaft, human or not, would ransack the vagina and fight the rear one for leeway. As she reconciled herself to the butt gouging her, she again fretted over – not the whips and appurtenances suspended on the far wall facing her – but Elodie's current rules governing a slave's right to orgasm when driven to that point under dire punishment. In any event, the whippings and tortures obviously awaiting her would bring her off, in spite of any dictates; if such entailed additional thrashings, why, she would just have to take them. And spend again.

Finally, Melanie seemed content with what she had taken such pains to prepare, the display presenting precisely what Elodie, and especially Anthea, had ordered – a completely nude and undeniably erotic, shapely body, chained outstretched, ringed, oiled, hooded, and, what was more (although Bouchard, while insisting the breast teats should be fully bloated, had not requested it), the crotch labia distended to their extreme reach. Melanie agreed from her own experience that a slave's vagina, about to be lashed, should be seen rather than merely presumed to be in full flood, and she said so.

"As this is the most sensitive, secluded and depraved part of a female," her bunched fingers squelched into the sopping oval, "it should be revealed for punishment – like that." She gave the clit ring a vicious upward tug that caused the week's offering to lurch back on the anal rod and expel a further dribble of juice into the void between the thighs.

*

Quite suddenly, the Marquise entered the sweltering precinct, accompanied by Anthea and the major-domo, all three veiled, the two women summarily cloaked. Freshly powdered with a beauty spot on a cheek, another gracing the curve of the left breast, Elodie seated herself regally in the single high-backed throne, the second chair, usually occupied by her husband, having been removed. The deferential Bouchard was heavily masked, as though in no way wishing to be reminded by the superb, appetizing body chained before the august company, of his part in the June drama; vengeance, in fact, clearly manifested itself in the form of his erection, the stupendous phallus throbbing visibly under the studded straps along its length. Gracefully, he helped the Marquise to divest herself of her velvet mantle; he did likewise for Anthea, who then, apart from her sandals and face veil, stood unclothed behind her aunt. There was nothing that delighted Elodie more than to watch her angelic, if bloodthirsty, niece flogging a stark naked, unusually heavy-breasted slave, both bodies tense, nude and sweating. Ah, that was rapture!

While Bouchard informed his three acolytes of the

slave's sentence decided upon at the dinner table, Joanne regarded through her hood's meagre eye-slits the two women whom, three months previously, she and Martine had caused to be put to the whip by the château servants. Now that she herself was about to suffer in the same way, and unquestionably far more unpleasantly, she regretted that she had not tried her hand in whipping them, at least this licentious niece with pert, upturned nipples. Closing her eyes, she recalled the thrill of last June when watching the pampered bitch being flagellated...

On her part, the Marquise felt it her legitimate right to proceed with what she and her niece, still beset with festering hatred for the slave, had hastily planned the previous night. Moreover, Elodie had made it clear to the château chaplain, Father Antoine, under the seal of the confessional, what they intended to mete out to 'the philistine parpaillote whore' who had so naively returned to Lassignac. Both women had readily received his benediction but thought it best he did not take part in the actual sessions, preferring he sat in, after sanctifying the scourges and implements, to watch and pray.

"So, my delectable infidel," Elodie purred, after a prolonged silence during which Bouchard and Melanie had the valet grease their whips, "we meet again. I'm sure you recognize this chamber – a place you used to frequent often enough in times past, did you not, whore? The furnishings, as well as some of the devices you see on yonder wall may be new to you, but believe me, you will get to know them soon enough – even though your solitary sojourn here will be brief before I sell you off in Toulon, as still is my intention. I say 'solitary' since I would not wish your presence, or what's left of you, to infect the souls and defile the bodies of my other inmates. I thought of ordering my major-domo, whom I have pardoned for last June, to bring in one or two of your erstwhile sisters, still serving me, to watch you suffer. But I have decided against it, for the very sight of what I am going to have done to you, will scare them into eternal submission and douse the fire in them." She paused, only to add, despondently, "You have truly grieved me, Joanne, for have I not housed, fed and indulged you in a manner few sluts of your humble origin have ever enjoyed? But now it is our turn to gratify ourselves."

She turned abruptly to her domestics. "Are the instruments in order and ready for use, you two? I want none of the usual delays in handing them to my niece when she starts work, whether tonight or on subsequent evenings. The needles, for instance, and flesh rakes... the chains and weights for the rings. And I assume you've oiled the whips on the panel over there." The jewelled fingers motioned towards the copious array of flogging leathers and crops dangling from hooks planted in the wallboards. The Sandrine creature halted her friggings a moment to assure her mistress that all was prepared. Indeed, she had spent well over an hour on the items, aware that the slightest dereliction of duty could entail a night, ankle-hung in the courtyard, and a mightily raw crotch after Coursel's use of the coach whip. Feeling she had satisfied her demanding owner, she reverted, Joanne noticed, to reviving her clit that had shrunk with fright when she was addressed.

Elodie then enquired of Anthea whether she wished

to add to the homily, at which the girl shook her head, her veiled eyes fixed upon the implement rack. The Marquise resumed addressing the slave: "You will spend the week down here, harlot, and suffer to a degree few of my flock have known. My major-domo and the dutiful Melanie will first flog you – and to that I shall lend full attention, for I have not forgotten how erotically you respond to the whip. Then my cherished niece here" – her thin, blue-veined hand gently caressed the girl's thigh – "will have carte blanche to do what she holds will improve your moral fibre." Again she stopped, drawing a deep breath as though bridling her desire to commence the evening's orgy, only to say, "Of course, my loyal servants will make unstinted use of that rich calyx you have between the thighs which, I'm pleased to see, has been unfurled." There Joanne caught sight of Melanie's smirk, as, whip in hand, she took up her stance behind her. "And by calyx I presume you know to what part of your whorish body I refer," the Marquise smiled. "But then, if I have understood what the duty guards tell me, that seems to be the principal object of your obscene lascivity, for apparently you abuse it several times a night. So, a good lashing and the visit of a strapped cock will not come amiss. And let me add, slummack, you may spend your vile curd as often and as plenteously as you like."

The Marquise settled herself more comfortably in her chair, sliding her thighs forward so that she could take her cunt and clit in hand. "Now, the two of you, beat this trollop to the blood! You, Bouchard, deal with the foremeat to start with, and Melanie, my sweet clit-licker, lay into those buttocks - yes, I know she's spigotted, but flay above and below the rod. Let us enjoy seeing you both turn that wealth of sirloin and belly into rare meat. We'll persecute the breasts and splayed vulva in sequence on each of the following nights. And I hope, Melodie, you've scented her body and orifices with the usual perfumes."

As the favourite assured her with a nod, the Marchioness's wigged head motioned to her junior menials to cease masturbating and pay attention to the candelabra, in case wax were needed for the body.

Simultaneously, the two scourges rose high before and to the rear of the column of naked flesh and descended into the loins and buttocks with a force that seemed almost to cut the victim in half. Joanne bore the first dozen lashes valiantly enough, the blows falling alternately, each methodically spaced from the next. In turn, the body was driven back on to the anal shaft and then impelled forwards, the slave's distended sphincter squelching in and out at each lunge. With sweat brimming inside the tight slave hood, the teeth bared and gritted as the septum ring chimed against them, her heroism, for which she had once been renowned, did not last long. The muffled moans and then the cries she uttered filled the precinct, along with the sound of each successive lash, as tears and blinding flashes of pain deprived the slave of sight through the narrow eye slits. Unaware of how many welts the two floggers were required by Elodie to raise on the rump, belly and thighs, the slave bore what she could in a dark cloud of submission… until suddenly the whipping ceased.

Vaguely, she heard Elodie's mocking yet quavering voice mingling with her own groans. "Feel the whore's lair of lechery, Bouchard. Is the sex-stump fully exposed from its sheath and well erect? If so, inform the bitch she can come, if she hasn't spent already. One can't tell with all this shrieking." With one hand clamped between her thighs, the other caressing Anthea's vulva, the aunt rallied herself. "Now, my loyal ones, prepare her for my patient niece to give that rancid crevice a lesson it will never forget." As the girl leaned down to kiss her aunt's cheek, she seemed to hear what she expected from Elodie. "I want the slut truly beaten before turning the body over to you, mon ange. But when the time comes, I expect you to lash hard into that cleft of crud that never seems to cease drooling. But remember, my Slave Master has to have his turn. Then we'll sling what's left of the bitch up from the rafter chains and make her truly repent. But now, my luscious Melodie, and you Bouchard, ripen the whore for my niece."

Hardly able to believe that still further sequences of real torment were to come, Joanne was conscious enough to wonder if indeed she could last out the night, let alone the week. As far as she could gather, this night would not see her suspended head down, with her legs drawn apart by the ankles. And yet the thought of what awaited her later caused her nipples to shrink into the refuge of the areoles, the ringed clitoris withdrawing into its protective sheath. She wondered how long her breasts would remain undamaged; with six further nights ahead under the women's ferocity, there was scant chance of their remaining unscathed, anymore than they could hope of escaping the effect of Bouchard's iron pincers.

As a further slew of lashes slammed into the lower

front and back regions, the slave strove to control her ascent towards further authorized but inescapable orgasms which were rapidly exhausting her.

Quite unexpectedly, after a murmured exchange between the two noblewomen, the Marquise again halted the ordeal with a curt order.

"The doxy's udders, Bouchard! They're slewing too freely for my liking. They need to stand firm and taut if they're to benefit fully from what my niece intends to enjoy later. Throttle those lolling bags of lymph, fellow! And, Anthea, ma douce, I want them well welted before you start on them. And we have to think of the spiked tongs. As to the needles, you'll have to wait until tomorrow, chérie. So, Bouchard, go ahead and clamp the slattern."

"With pleasure, my lady," the perspiring flogger panted, "but I gathered the tit-tie was foreseen for tomorrow's session. I mean, for the pincers and bodkins. Have I misunderstood Your Grace's orders?"

"Do as I say, man. Clamp them tight at the roots. It vexes me to see such bales of suet swinging so insolently. Anyway, they can do with a foretaste of what awaits them anon." She turned to her Anthea as Sandrine handed the long flesh-crop to the young vixen of a niece. "You'd prefer them trussed up, wouldn't you, mon trésor?"

Joanne saw Anthea nod, her veiled countenance and graceful neck already flushed with pleasure.

Painstakingly, the major-domo encircled the root of each sagging breast with the horrendous metal brace and screwed the jaws tight, so that the strangled bulges could be worked on at ease. (Joanne recalled from slave gossip in her former time of imprisonment that the irons had been the gift of a Spanish Inquisitor visiting France and advising how best to stamp out heresy.) As the crescents of tines embedded into the soft blubber, the slave let out a gasp of pain; although accustomed to having her overweighted bubs garrotted, never had she been made to experience the penetration of prongs. Striving against the collar flange forcing her head aloft, she could see her breasts pointing and resembling fire-red projectiles from a culverin, except that they had turned purple, the colour of Burgundy. The areoles and teats bulged, engorged, the veins throbbing under the skin like worms trying to escape. Whenever her precious milk churns had been strangled with cord and beaten, it proved almost a pleasure, but the iron semicircles were very different. And her balconies feared the needles; the niece was not going to content herself by merely skewering the tits but would probably thrust the longest bodkins directly into the nipple vents. But what again scared her was the subsequent, agonizing release of the mounds and the circulation taking up again. She only hoped she would be able to reach orgasm under the whips before the clamps were removed.

Elodie's instructions to her four retainers were, however, far from over. "I trust, good Bouchard, you took careful note of what my niece and I decided at table, regarding what we wish this pig of a parpaillote to undergo, once her outlandishly gross bosoms have been dealt with. It would be fitting to inform your two underlings of our decision so that the punishments proceed without unseemly delay." Promptly, Deljoux and Sandrine ceased masturbating, as their overseer nodded and addressed them.

"The Marquise desires the slave to be positioned otherwise for the evening's ensuing sequence. You will release the strumpet's legs, attach the ankles to those farther chains over there," – he gestured to lengths of links attached to hooks set in the opposite wall, some way behind him – "and be sure to part the whore's limbs wide, without – and harken, both of you – dislocating the haunch sockets. Our exalted ladies wish to have full access to the bitch's crotch, and you know how they like to see the thigh muscles in tension. So make sure both pairs of ringed labia are splayed by the shackling you'll pass round the hips and join to the dildo in her rectum. Just as we did when stretching out that turbulent, blonde wench we had to deal with a week ago." Joanne wondered who that victim had been and if she knew her.

The two assistants bowed, clearly delighted to be charged with setting up yet another condemned slave for what they particularly liked to watch, Sandrine having suffered similar but milder treatment in the past: horizontal bondage, crotch flogging and penetration of the gaping vagina, and possibly the anus, if freed from the rear rod. The throat would also be available for use. Assisting with similar torments inflicted a while back, both menials had truly relished each stage of such punishments, watching their Master's studded, rawhide-braided phallus gouging into a writhing slave – a slattern who had just been whipped with salutary force to curb her overindulgent frigging. The present victim, from what they had gathered from Melodie, was to be flogged far more fiercely, and for reasons other than merely sexual.

Elodie listened attentively to her major-domo

repeating her own orders but seemed irritated, once he had finished, when the skimpily-attired Sandrine, always eager for commendation and promotion, had the effrontery to enquire whether the anal rod should be removed, when the body was levelled out.

"Of course not, you dolt," the Marquise shrilled back. "Deljoux has only to extend the brank further out. And if you don't watch that wagging tongue of yours, I'll have the rod rammed into your maw

and lash your fat arse to the quick."

The thickset cow of a slave handler, to Joanne's contentment, turned white, apologizing humbly and glancing nervously at the knotted scourges Bouchard and Melanie still had in hand, the leathers dripping with slave sweat. To make amends and beg pardon for her pointless remark, the slut hurried to kneel before her mistress's parted thighs, only to be kicked aside and ignored.

A moment later, Joanne felt the links holding her arms being extended down and the ankles released. It was Deljoux who then drew the legs forward, clipping the bondage straps to chains extended from the opposite wall. She found her body stretched almost parallel to the floor and held aloft by the anal rod, now at its full length and still firmly rooted in the rectum. Before her head slumped back between the arms, she caught sight of the two seniors conversing with Elodie and Anthea. What was said lay beyond her hearing but it was accompanied by veiled glances towards her and, to the slave's amazement, by Anthea calmly running a gloved hand up and down Bouchard's erection, the aunt merely smiling, seeming more interested in the folds of Melanie's saturated vulva.

Plainly, the session so far had been edifying for Elodie. Whatever was now to follow would, Joanne suspected, delight the woman even further – and if the whips buried deep into the crotch, the victim was meant to enjoy it equally.

With her legs wrenched wide and harnessed to the wall cleats, Joanne feared for her joints and, above all, for her open groin. And with reason, for Deljoux was already drawing the labia apart with further chains that encircled the thighs and sank into the welted buttock meat behind; tugging on the ends, he coupled them to the summit of the extended shaft impaling the slave's rear. The way in which the wet vagina yawned was a clear beckoning to those entrusted by the Marquise with its punishment. Yet Joanne's head sank down submissively between the arms and, noticing again how near the instruments on the wall seemed to be, the superb length of flesh and muscle resigned itself to fate. Suddenly she tensioned, catching sight of Bouchard standing between her outstretched legs, whip unfurled. Caressing his strapped erection, the man gazed from behind his mask at the leaking cunt and the clitoris skinned of its protective sleeve – which Joanne felt merited something more solid than just a slack whip thong… As to Melanie, she had stationed herself a lash length's distance from the hollowed sweep of the belly and jutting rib cage, as if eager to show her Mistress again how she too was able to draw blood like Bouchard.

The Marquise then repeated and confirmed what the slave had already heard.

"I have no objection, trollop, from now on, to you spilling your bawdy juices when you spend. It will only sap the strength you'll need to cope with what I'm going to have done to you over the next nights. So, please yourself. Make use of my benevolence as you wish. Spurt out that foul slush while you're whipped, as you used to do. Or you can remain inert. It's of no importance to me. But knowing your licentious nature, to climax may help you to endure what Anthea, my major-domo and Melanie are going to inflict on your depraved, reprobate body. Now, apostate infidel, prepare that crotch of yours to expiate the crime you brazenly perpetrated at my expense." The words she used bewildered the slave.

At that, the victim felt Bouchard wrest her clit ring almost out of its piercing. She let out a stifled cry and, on the verge of orgasm, controlled herself and her fright – for something far worse than penance was leaning over her masked face. The niece's vulva gleamed directly before the hood's mouth slit. That was what she saw; what she felt was the tail end of the scourge drifting menacingly over her pubic mound. Joanne almost puked when her ringed nose caught the cloying smell of the bitch's crotch; it nauseated her, but not for long. The perineum bore down on to the leather and stopped up the nostrils.

Then Anthea rasped out the inevitable order. "Slurp me out, whore, and woe if you don't satisfy me time and time again while I bloat that cunt of yours. Dally or retch and I'll have you stretched on that crucifix yonder and I'll rake, whip and…and… que Dieu te garde…I'll…I'll devastate you. So, slut, to work with that studded tongue of yours, the same forked appendage as that between the Devil's jaws!"

The woman seemed to have taken leave of her senses

but Joanne's compliant tongue emerged from the narrow leather slot and, after licking the labia, managed to reach the bared clitoris and suck it in. As the cunnilingus began, Anthea's riding whip slashed down into the outstretched, drooling oval of what the niece condemned as 'Great Satan's squalid lair of lust'. "Ventre de Dieu," she swore, "I'll flay this damn strumpet raw!" Not to the aunt's displeasure, the niece embarked on her vengeance with resolve.

Stoically, the slave endured the crotch whipping, delivered with a crop bound in horsehide, as long as she was able before descending into a mist of oblivion, her mouth behind the hood unable to swallow more of the niece's discharges. If the sweating Anthea paused occasionally as she was tongued off, the cane continued to fall, sending Joanne climaxing through one spasm after another, her muffled gasps lost among the slushings. The treat – or rather, ordeal – dispensed by the château favourite was compounded, at long last, by Melanie's merciless lashes over the clamped breasts. The victim was despatched into a vortex of sex, vicious pain and orgiastic bliss that only a submissive slave can know.

It was only when a well-satisfied, sweltering Anthea had returned to her aunt's side that Bouchard was given his turn. Depositing his scourge on the concave belly, he veered his gleaming cutlass of a phallus downwards and slid it smoothly into the scabbard of mucilage – these being some of Elodie's favourite similes. Plundering such leeway as the anal dildo left available, the cock dome butted the rod lodged beyond the thin membrane separating the two inner tracts. Joanne suddenly revived, moaning with gathering pleasure, and jerking her haunches aloft, as far as her chains allowed, to ride the erection. A dozen thrusts brought her off again, even more vehemently than under the whips; and finally, in the grip of ecstasy, she felt the penis tense, pause and pump her vagina full of that boiling, turbid sperm – or what Marie-Félice called 'clotted curd' – that every Lassignac inmate supped on regularly at least twice a night.

Even Elodie was bewitched, watching her naked penitent writhe, and content to hear the groans stifling within the slave hood. Though the cries of pleasure were irrelevant, they had humoured the Marquise as she put an end to that evening's punishments, noticing the slave's stamina waning when the body was released and chained to the wall, the arms stretched up backwards behind the shoulder blades.

As the contented company departed, the valet duly extracted the ribbed dildo from the rectum and cranked it back in place against its bracket, before ripping the sopping slave hood off the head and face. Muttering to himself, he unshackled the vandalized breasts, returning the root clamps to their hooks on the instrument board. As the globes of mammary meat swung free to hang pendulously and resume their former shape, Joanne again wailed at the pain caused by the blood flowing back into them; she continued to moan until Deljoux soused the bags of flogged breast flesh with water from a nearby keg.

"Now, whore, weep away through what's left of a steamy night," the thug told her, slapping the livid, welted bulges of what he ominously termed 'brothel blubber ripe for branding'. "A few nights more and these flabby balconies will have lost some of their bulk, if you want to trust what Melanie says. I'll stake a wager you've never been chained by the dugs to the flogging post, eh, bitch? Or – see that rafter hook yonder? – hung by a chain round the roots..." The girl was too far gone to muster a reply; all she wanted, damn him, was to be left to sleep and rest her sinews for the nights still to come.

After being given a drink of the same polluted liquid from the keg, hardly enough to quench her thirst, the candles doused, the brazier coals hissing when the lout pissed on them, Joanne was left in total darkness. Thinking of her Marquis, Francis-Etienne, she lamented his absence, for he most likely would have curbed much of his wife's vindictiveness. Why he, many leagues away, should now suddenly come to mind mystified Joanne but, under the circumstances, her strict bondage forestalling any hope of masturbating, about whom else could she fantasize? For want of anything better, she made do with the memory of the evening's orgasms the whips had brought about, which compensated to some degree...

*

She guessed it was quite late the following day when preparations for the further punishments began. Meanwhile, she had been molested only twice since waking – first by Melanie, who taunted her and, extending the wrist chains, made her stoop and lick her off, Joanne finding the woman tasted far less tart than Anthea. The other, quite gratuitous, harassment was from Deljoux; completely against the rules, he simply thrashed her and, just as Melanie had done, lowered her to have himself sucked off. (Joanne swore to herself that she would somehow make him regret his insolence.)

Suddenly, however, when Sandrine appeared, straight from bed and for once unveiled, Joanne sensed that something strange was afoot. Lanthorn in hand, the portly wench stepped cautiously across the straw-strewn tiles, putting a finger to her lips. Instinct told Joanne that the visit was in some way clandestine, for the tense face did not have the usual impassive expression the subordinate wore when on precinct duty, greasing the whips, oiling the rusty flesh rakes and tending the brazier with the bellows.

"You have a visitor," she murmured, "all the way from Paris. Someone we all know and she wants me to bring her down here. Why, God knows. But not a word to Deljoux, Coursel or even a maid, let alone Melanie and the mighty ones. She has a message for you." With that, she returned to the iron-bracketed door she had left ajar and beckoned.

Who should enter, clad in velvet riding breeches and mired boots, but Marie-Félice, Elodie's most dependable and vicious flogger of earlier times, prior to the Marquis taking her with him to Paris. The masked apparition astonished Joanne, besides raising terror in her guts, though the woman carried no riding crop nor that metal-lugged switch which could split open a buttock with a mere dozen lashes.

The former slave mistress spoke in a hushed voice. "The Marquis has learned of your return here, you reckless idiot. The news reached us through gossip on the part of the rider who apparently brought you back when you were being carted north. Someone – Dieu sait qui – must have passed a message to our most distinguished Marquis at court" – Joanne noticed the gracious epithet identifying her owner. "Rumours, fair or foul, travel rapidly here, you know. Anyway, he's already on his way, travelling south by royal coach, a day behind me. He ordered me to seek you out and inform you that he'll be here anon. Meanwhile you'll have to endure whatever his wife is doing to you – the sort of things that, knowing you, you're probably enjoying – until he arrives, probably late this evening. Like me, he's travelling day and night. Now, I have to go. My pretext for being here is to collect his hunting horn and second musket."

As stealthily as she had appeared, the Master's concubine, currently flaunting her charms – and wielding her whip – among the nobility at Court, left with Sandrine, also sworn to secrecy and who received disdainful looks from the Paris visitor. Praying that what she had just heard might possibly be true rather than trumped up (Marie-Félice being among France's most accomplished liars, who were innumerable), Joanne could not believe what had just been said or the manner in which it had been conveyed. Although excited by the girl's news, she wondered how this provincial whore, even if the mistress to a titled aristocrat, could possibly have been entrusted with such a mission.

The extraordinary incident over, and Marie-Félice no doubt being assigned a bedroom and a stable for her mount, the slave had to prepare for her second evening of penance that promised to be far worse than the first. She supposed the former slave mistress would be invited to share in the whippings but truly hoped not, for in her time the woman had ranked among the château's fiercest floggers. And should no Marquis be on his way, she doubted whether, with Marie-Félice in residence and solicited to partake with that muscular arm of hers, not even a hardened slave would last out a week.

*

Having supped on leftovers and been given a mug of wine, Joanne was again hooded up and chained in a position she had never really liked: stretched, rump up, by the arms and legs fully parted to four lengths of chain descending from the precinct's central beams, and the neck flange forcing her head backwards. The posture might appear erotic to an overseer but Joanne, as far as her buttocks and drooping breasts were concerned, had known less painful positions, many of which she had enjoyed immensely. But her months at Lassignac had accustomed her to accept without question what the dominant rather than the submissive wanted, aware that a slave, deprived of choice, relinquished herself far more readily to the whip. However, it perturbed her that her welted breasts were left to sway invitingly and loose.

Though a long, if fitful, sleep had refreshed her, one of the bizarre artefacts she saw through her mask slits also made her fret: Bouchard had inserted a metal ring at the point where the foreskin gathered to join the bulb on the underside of his penis. The circlet glinted threateningly and since obviously it would chafe the clitoris, if the slave was fucked from behind, as it was trawled in and out with each thrust of the man's cock, the bared sex stud would be abraded and ground to a gristle in no time. Moreover, from earlier episodes in the year in the slave cellar she knew that a grommet, cock ring or strapping always brought her off far too rapidly, cheating her of the gradual measured climaxes she usually enjoyed. But again, how could she, a mere whip-wench, choose how she wished her subservient body to be used? A slave took what she was given.

As though sensing her anxieties, Bouchard slapped each of her drooping, welted bubs, first forehand across the left bag of offal, and then, with a studded backhand, hard into the other. Joanne groaned under the usual melange of pain and compliance, her breasts still aching from what they had already suffered. As now they hung directly downwards, she realized how enticing they must seem to a connoisseur, carrying out what at Lassignac was known as 'bust basting'; she only hoped her teats would not bleed; at least, luckily, they would not spurt milk like, Joanne recalled, that pregnant slave from the Rouergue back in May when she had her mammaries put into the throttling vice to receive the rattan cane.

The major-domo grasped the sagging burdens that he considered, given his erotic partialities, among the best he'd had the pleasure of working on. As he stretched them down as far as they would reach from the gashed roots, Joanne caught the malicious smile behind his veil and trusted they would not be irremediably damaged, and thus jeopardize her future when carted off to one of Elodie's port brothels.

Bowing to his revered owner, the man confirmed that the slung nude was ready for sentencing.

"Tonight, our wanton betrayer, we shall really teach you fidelity," Elodie thereupon informed her victim. "Once I've had the lower crevices and those heretical udders well beaten, we shall see how they take to my new set of honed bodkins, a thoughtful gift presented to me recently by my dear friend, Evelyn de Burre-Sage, whom you certainly remember. They enter the bubs, labia and pubic mound most pleasingly and the sapphire-jewelled hilts, when firmly in place, glint like angels' eyes. Of course, you've had similar ones thrust in before, but not these. As you have the faculty of serendipity, you're sure to enjoy them." The strange, foreign term scared Joanne. "So, Anthea and Melanie, my two sweet wenches, and you, Bouchard, kindly proceed."

Joanne had endured, with or without pleasure, numberless beatings in her time but what the Marquise had her Anthea and the slave mistress inflict on the curved back, purple rump and up into the vulva surpassed anything the slave had known. But it was rather the opulence of the 'drudge's dugs' – as Elodie was given to calling Joanne's drooping sacks – that especially delighted Melanie who said they swung like 'her favourite goat's udders at milking time.' Already Bouchard was in his element, raising further welts, first on the front of the suspended cones and ringed teats, and then, changing place with Melanie, excelling himself by flaying the rear cambers of swinging meat with the bamboo rod. Elodie, who in her time had exerted much diligence in training all three floggers, or at least the two women, gave herself what she declared later to have been a 'well-deserved orgasm she would not forget'.

Once the Marquise considered the sites adequately welted, Bouchand was ordered to pierce the whinging victim, a pastime he revelled in also, particularly if

Her Ladyship was present. He took the bodkins from a cut glass vase of mauve liquid, proffered by Sandrine, and one by one some dozen or so spikes traversed the vulval lappets, one passing through the summit of the clitoris, above the ring. He then drove a further handful into the flaccid, pendant breasts, the silver lengths catching the candlelight as they puckered the skin and slid slowly in. Each jab brought a hiss from behind the slave hood and then a long sigh; the reaction to the longer needles piercing the nipple ducts, as expected, was more of a groan than the sharp yelp the man expected; yet it rose to the rafters all the same, the retainers thoroughly enjoying the session that constituted part payment for their exertions.

The interminable evening concluded with Bouchard using the bullwhip on the buttocks rather than the supple cane, with the cherished Vonnange niece taking the slave mistress's place opposite him to thrash the thighs to the blood with her riding crop. Weak from tension, the insertions and lashes, Joanne surrendered and slumped, but not before careering through a final blinding orgasm. How long she remained slung from the chains, neither the departed Elodie nor her niece would know, for well after midnight it was none other than Marie-Félice still in riding habit, and summoned by Sandrine, who reappeared. Together the two extracted the needles, released the slave and, with the Parisienne giving the orders, spread-eagled the spent body to recover on the marking bench – an item listed on Elodie's agenda for use two days later, when the pubis would receive the red-hot branding iron.

*

The third day had already dawned outside the precinct, but of that the exhausted nude was unaware, just as she could not know the Marquis's coachman, still leagues away, had with a louis prevailed upon a young local peasant to take to horse and alert Marie-Félice of her master's imminent arrival, soon after first light – hence the reason for the woman being up at cockcrow and on the qui vive. To Sandrine's surprise and alarm, the concubine ordered her to remove the slave's septum ring and rub salve into the welts and the sites where the needles had entered the slave's flesh. Returning to life, Joanne was grateful for the relief but could not believe anyone would dare take such steps without Elodie's sanction or at least agreed to by Bouchard. Strange things indeed were taking place.

Quite abruptly, on being given a shabby cape, the exhausted victim of the precinct's second night was told by Marie-Félice to spruce herself up. "The Marquis will soon be here and you'd better try to look your best, as he would expect. The coach will then probably leave once he has refreshed himself, had the horses watered and the driver fed. It's a long trek back to Paris, and you must think of the trouble we've gone to in coming down here." Again Joanne could not be sure she was hearing aright: Francis-Etienne himself, like Marie-Félice, again present before her in person under the eaves of the Château Lassignac! And this talk of Paris…! As the girl had said, news spreads speedily in the kingdom, with so many eager tongues and ears about.

What to Joanne seemed like a century later, a second lampion illuminated the confines of Elodie's secret retreat. With a petrified Sandrine bowing low, Marie-

Félice ushered in none other than the Marquis de Vonnange-Lassignac. First, he stared at the stakes, chains and implements thronging what once had been his sanctum, and only then at what confronted him, the denuded beauty now perched on the margin of the stone block. He summoned his concubine forward, as though about to avenge himself on someone, at the same time grasping the pommel of his rapier – rather than the bulge of his noble cock perceptible within the deerskin breeches. He seemed strangely taken aback, frowning and stroking his pointed beard.

"She is not adequately clothed for the journey, wench. Fetch the necessary from the old raiment closet above." At that, the one who had travelled ahead of him calmly gestured to the half-clothed Sandrine, who scurried out to unearth what she could from the Marquise's rosewood wardrobe, one of the many cluttering the château. "Then have Fremont ready the horses," the man called after her, at the same time as telling his bed whore, "We return to Versailles at once. Seat the girl next to you in the coach."

"Shall I summon Madame la Marquise to the courtyard for the departure, master?" the slender, leather-coated tart enquired, to which she received a look that Joanne, now standing with her bruised thighs flattened against the slab, felt was that of someone who would not have been averse to bending his concubine back over the stone, descending her breeches and either beating or fucking her. But clearly he was anxious to be gone. "Attend to your duties, wench," the questioner was told. "There is no need of any adieux. But see to it we have provisions and wine from the kitchens. Our first night's stop will be at the hostelry outside St. Flour." All of a sudden, he added, "In the coach, I want the slave to sit with her thighs well parted, so that I may look upon her ringed crotch and sagging labia which please me greatly…"

The kept paramour gave a jaundiced look but also sauntered off, flaunting her buttocks – as though showing Joanne how a Marquis's mistress could also seduce her owner – leaving the man for the first time alone with the unclad object of his journey. Thereupon he addressed the slave directly.

"I am indeed pleased, Joanne, to meet up with you again," he murmured, motioning her forward to stand before him and refusing to let her go to her knees in deference. "We'll have that fine body of yours shipshape soon enough, once you are out of here. But, mark my words – from now on, you will be under the orders of my mistress, Marie-Félice, whenever I am absent at court. You will defer to her without question, just as you do to me. It matters not whether you're whipped by her or by me, I now being the sole proprietor of your person and body. You will obey instantly, though you will be relatively free within my lodgings, despite my keeping you stark naked and chained. But when I invite certain visitors of an evening to sup and amuse themselves at cards, you will serve them submissively, as is your way. Knowing you well, that will not displease you, nor will my bedposts and certain other features chez moi that Marie-Félice is well acquainted with and will show you on arrival. And," he added, after a pause, his eyes on Joanne's capacious, welted breasts, "our floggings will be frequent and pleasing." The slave smiled, bowed low and murmured softly her usual "Thank you, Master".

A moment later, the three figures met up with the coachman in the courtyard just as the sun was rising, and took their places in the sumptuous phaeton. Partially draped in the ragged cloak and desperately trying to disregard the pain besetting her welted bottom and thighs, Joanne was seated next to Marie-Félice who was ordered to remove the slave's neck flange and attend to some of the more sombre abrasions the lashings had left on the breasts and lower regions. As the horses moved off with a jolt, the coach wheels rumbling over the lowered drawbridge Joanne had so imprudently traversed only some days before, she looked back at the forbidding château. Quite distinctly, she caught sight of Elodie and the anathema of a niece peering down from a lancet in the northern tower at what was taking place before their eyes: the further 'desertion' of a prisoner with whom they had, alackaday, far from finished…

Of Bouchard and Melanie there was no sign. Perhaps wisely they would have sought sanctuary, Joanne supposed, in the major-domo's inviolable, private quarters, preferring a soft bed to confronting the Marquise too soon under the prevailing circumstances. What would now befall the other inmates down in the cellars, by way of revenge, the departing slave did not wish to imagine. She could almost hear the crack of whips and the cries…

*

The long but delightful journey north in a coach that, emblazoned with the royal arms, passed without hindrance each octroi on the route, was pure rapture for the one cuddled up next to the salacious, if wary,

Marie-Félice. The favourite seemed pleased at having a sister paramour to share her days – and particularly nights – and with whom she could gossip in the patois common to them both. However, their owner told them to use correct French, being interested to learn what had become of the attractive wench since that most unfortunate month of June. Joanne was careful to recount only some of the facts and, with Marie-Félice all ears, not her real reason for her 'romantic' return to the château. It would have surprised the Marquis.

Little of note took place at the various overnight sojourns at inns and noble residences en route, apart from slurpings and yowls occasioned by the girls who were allowed to share a bed, while their wearied Marquis slept apart. Yet, the nightly indulgences in what he took to be seemingly endless bouts of cunnilingus amused their owner. But once Marie-Félice was asleep, Joanne meditated on what awaited her in Paris, once lodged in the Versailles apartments of the one to whom she presumed she now exclusively belonged. She also wondered if, once deprived of her travelling cloak and obliged to live naked, she would be allowed to keep her six remaining flesh rings and the stud in her tongue in place. For in a way, she would regret losing them.

***

Unless a further screed in Joanne's scrawl comes to light, it is not possible to recount the subsequent months of her existence, slogging away as a nobleman's second 'sufferer-in-residence', amid Marie-Félice's sudden fits of jealousy and pique. Nor can one speculate on the treatment meted out to the 'parpaillote' by the Marquis and his associates, ably assisted by the suddenly 'promoted' mistress, whose biceps, Joanne found, had lost none of their strength.

One rumour, however, has come down to us, from which it appears that the newcomer was to become the thin edge of the wedge that eventually dislodged Marie-Félice from her privileged status in the Marquis's entourage. What consequences this had can only be surmised.

In any event, Paris proved to be no Garden of Eden. As the preacher in her earlier days in Geneva was wont to say, 'no one can enjoy eternal peace and pleasure in this evil world'. That was an utterance a beautiful, sexually-gifted country lass, wearing nipple and genital rings and nothing else, found to be true enough.

Much of the above was taken from a tattered MS marked 'Versailles, the 16th of November, 1702' Caroline has also written;

Eliska

Beaucastel

Castle of Torment

The Sufferers

Silvana's Quest

Puritan Punishment

Parisian Punishment

Illustrated versions of some of her books are available from the Readers' Club. See end of book for details.

SLAVE.

BY SEAN O'KANE

Sean's erotic fiction typically features strong plots and strong characters. Here he offers the reader an atmospheric piece and a very alluring heroine.

"What's her name?" James asks.

"She doesn't need one," Mcloud replies. "I usually keep her close enough that clicking my fingers is adequate." The older man takes a deep draw on his cigar.

"Make more drinks, you useless slut," he says, settling back on his sunlounger and holding up his now drained glass of Pimms.

James watches the nameless slave as she curtsies to her master, takes the glass from her master and then approaches him. He holds up his own glass. She takes it and for a moment their fingers touch. Her bones feel slight and delicate, her skin smooth and soft. Suddenly he has doubts.

"Last week, at the club, you said she could take anything a master could throw at her............." He lets his doubts hang in the summer air as he watches her walk back into the house. Her back is slender and graceful – he has to admit that the shoulders look quite adequate for withstanding the whip, but her waist is so trim he feels his hands could encircle it. Her hips and buttocks are sensational, almost out of proportion in their luxuriance, at every step in her high heeled sandals the buttocks tremble temptingly beneath the thin fabric of her teal shift dress.

"I did. And I meant it. If you're a seriously interested buyer then you're welcome to try her out here and now. Anything you like. Clamps, needles, any type of whip, wax, humiliation, objectification, fuck, buggery and fellation. All yours my boy……..if you've got the money."

"I've got it," James assures the older man. The blonde slave is returning, holding the two replenished glasses. James notes her legs; long and well-shaped – not catwalk perfect but possessing the two most important elements of all – they are here and they are available.

He notices that she has a charming dusting of freckles on her cheeks beneath her grey-green eyes.

"Why are you selling her?" he asks.

"As I said old boy; even the best slavemeat gets boring after a while. Now, if you're serious, it's time we got down to work."

The blonde has placed the glasses on the table between the two men and now stands a few feet back, eyes demurely downcast, hands clasped in front of her at her groin. James notices her chest heaving as she breathes nervously. The dress is not daring but it does hint at broad, full swells of breast. As he watches he smiles. Her nipples have suddenly started to peak, she must know that she will be required for service shortly and is responding quite correctly.

"You are to do exactly what this gentleman tells you until I tell you differently, do you understand you worthless lump of whipping trash?"

James notices the slave's nipples swell into even harder prominence as she registers the invective from her master.

"Yes, Master." Her voice is gentle and cultured.

"Kneel before your master and worship him with your tongue until I tell you to take him into your mouth," James orders.

"Nice one," Mcloud acknowledges and unzips his flies to pull out his semi-tumescent cock. "That's pretty well the only thing the daft bitch is crap at, so I always do it for her," he says, settling back again as the blonde kneels beside him and leans forward.

Her pink tongue darts out, almost cat like and flicks at the shaft which twitches and throbs in response. Again she leans in, steadying herself on the edge of the lounger. Now she takes long slow licks and Mcloud's cock straightens, throbs, fills, until it stands proudly rigid, dwarfing the girl's face. Now she cups his scrotum through the material of his trousers and continues her long sensual licks, her tongue roving across the shiny dome of the helm, lingering at the slit that divides it.

"Now suck him and finish him," James orders and watches closely as the girl leans farther in, her pretty lips stretched wide, slowly she manages to encompass the impressive bulk of her master's penis and goes to work. Her hand clenches around the shaft and begins to slowly pump it. Her head sinks down, and then down again. James knows he can rival Mcloud for size of cock and is impressed with the smoothness of the blonde's technique. After he has whipped her and played with her, he will see what her mouth feels like. Mcloud reaches down and holds his slave's head tightly against him then bucks his hips urgently. Her rhythm doesn't alter at all. Calmly she continues to milk him with her hand while her throat works steadily at containing the thick fluid being jetted hard into her small mouth.

James clicks his fingers and stands, hurriedly the slave cleans her master's helm and stands up too, still swallowing, her tongue flicks at her lips tasting the final traces of sperm. He picks up her collar and lead from the table and holds them out. She takes them and buckles the collar on tightly, shakes her hair out and then resumes her submissive pose.

"She's a well trained bitch, James," Mcloud's voice is distant and content after his orgasm. "Use the summer house for a whipping if you like, she's fairly quiet. I'd use the playroom indoors if you want to pierce her and clamp her though. She can get noisy if the session goes on for long enough."

James picks up the riding crop lying on the table and uses the keeper to toy with her nipples now pressing urgently against her dress.

"Strip," he says.

There is just the dress and once she has stepped clear of it, puddled on the ancient flagstones of the terrace, she is wearing only a thong and her high heels. Her body is every bit as good as James had imagined and Mcloud's asking price seems now quite reasonable. She has obviously tanned topless and her breasts are the same dusky gold as the rest of her, the straining nipples a pleasing dark red on tawny, smooth areola.

"Cup them," he tells her. Her small hands immediately rise to support the neat breasts, he notes that she keeps her fingers well under the curve of flesh, making no move to hide or shield the nipples, just offer them up. Well trained indeed.

He steps back and lands two crisp strikes with the keeper across the nipples. Two charming intakes of breath follow on the slave's part but she still makes no move to shield herself. James taps his thigh with the crop and she drops to all fours, crawling to come alongside where the shaft is tapping his leg.

In the hot summer afternoon James strolls across the grass, towards the cedar trees, loosely he holds the loop of the leash and the crop in one hand. Sometimes he stops and looks down. The slave is magnificent from this angle, the wide hindquarters swelling dramatically from the slender waist, the buttock cleft, emphasised by the thong, beckoning to the crop to introduce itself to the seat of her femininity and her slavery. James jerks on her lead to stop her, then bends down behind her and wrenches the flimsy thing from out of her crease, tearing the waist straps and ripping it off.

Sarah holds herself steady, entirely comfortable with the knowledge that a master has the right to inspect, beat or fuck his slave's cunt at any time. The grass is cool under her knees and palms, the cedars make shifting veil-like patterns on it as they sway in the light breeze. Somewhere down in the village, hidden by a wooded hill, a motorbike snarls but cannot disturb the peace. She can almost feel this new master's breath on her hot, tingling vulva, she likes the look of him and is quite content to move on from her current master. She knows that every master is an adventure and she is keen to experience another man's mastery. In this new master – she hopes that is what he will be – she has detected an intriguing mixture of cruelty and sensuality. Very different to her present master's unsubtle and overbearing approach.

Suddenly she feels fingers stroking her labia and effortlessly slipping between their moist softness, she bites her tongue against the urge to mew with pleasure as she feels her inner tissues stroked and rubbed then tested by fingers being clenched. Similarly she fights against the urge to wag her bottom, she knows her cunt well enough to know that it will be doing all the talking that's needed and the new master's hand will exit her body with plenty of evidence of her submission to his examination. Suddenly the fingers are gone and she feels the warm wetness of them wiped on her left buttock, immediately the breeze begins to chill it on her skin.

"You're a fine looking creature, whatever your name is," Sarah hears him say from above and hides a smile beneath her thickly cascading blonde hair. He will find her name out soon enough – her master is just having his little joke. He bends down and grasps her right breast. It is the grip of a real master – not a lover – his hand weighs her tit, moves it, squeezes it. Between the fingers the nipple engorges even further and she cannot restrain a gasp of delicious pain as the rubbery tube is cruelly compressed. She knows from experience that her nipples are good ones for a slave – her previous master stretched them, then her present one took advantage of their length to introduce her to the delights of needle play. What will this one do if he buys her?

He clicks his fingers and smacks her bottom with the crop. They resume their progress towards the summerhouse and the whips and restraints it contains.

"The perfect position for breast whipping is when the slave's body cannot mitigate the lashes' effectiveness by any backward movement," he tells her once her back is up against the chill stone and her wrists and ankles are securely shackled to the steel rings set in them. She glances down and proudly notes that, although the air is warm, her nipples have hardened even further at the prospect of the whip. While he has been rummaging through the contents of the punishment box, an old oaken chest standing in the far corner, she has luxuriated in the tight bondage of the restraints and the movement of the air against her nakedness. She especially revels in the way the air caresses her between her wide spread legs, the exhibitionist in her writhes in delight as she glances out of the open French windows, across the lawn and towards the old wall that runs along the foot of the hill that hides her master's house so perfectly, and which allows her to be enjoyed nakedly and openly.

The new master approaches her with a heavy flogger. Her blood pounds as she studies the familiar, flat bladed lashes. It has always made her tits dance and swing with the clubbing weight of its blows, sending spears of excitement coursing through her. But best of all has been the look of wild delight on the master's face as he savours the sight of the havoc it caused on his slave's helpless body.

After twenty lashes, Sarah knows she wants this man to buy her. Her chest is burning, her breasts are hot and stinging – her nipples straining ever harder towards the next lash and the next. But then he stops and plunges his hand straight up into her. His thrust is arrogantly sure of itself, there is no conception of any possibility she might not be ready for him. He simply slams his hand straight into the hot wetness of her vulva. His fingers clench and she arches her back, thrusting her pelvis forward to meet the thumb that now grinds her clitoris and sends her headlong into orgasm.

"Your master's right." From a distance Sarah hears the new master's voice as she surfaces from the depths of masochistic heaven. "You don't need a name, you're just a body for anyone to use. Slut, whoreslave, bitch on heat, whipping meat."

She groans her pleasure at hearing the insults from a master.

Five minutes later she is preparing for the next part of the session. Now her wrists are clipped to the chain which hangs from the centre of the ceiling, she wipes her sweat-matted hair on her raised biceps, tries to stop her spread legs from trembling in post orgasmic spasm and hollows her back, ready for the stock whip. She knows without being told that she must stand with legs apart and back hollowed. The whip will be heavy and she will need to have her legs parted to hold as steady as she can under the beating. Her back must be hollowed to allow the master sight of her cunt as he laces her buttocks with thin lines of fiery agony, each one overlaying the previous one before she can finish absorbing the pain, so that she dances and twists and groans – and maybe makes the odd scream echo around the old stone of the summer house. She looks around and sees the new master has stripped to the waist. His body is lean and toned. The pectorals shift excitingly as he sweeps the long, pliable lash in front of him a couple of times to get the feel of it. He surprises her by looking up and their eyes meet. He smiles and she lowers her eyes instantly.

"I'll stop the beating when you're marked to my

satisfaction. Then I'll continue it for ten more strokes in punishment for that. Understand?" he tells her and she is pleased to note the hoarseness of excitement entering his voice. She knows she looks good, naked and in chains. She is certain he will beat her ferociously and then buy her.

"Yes, master," she says and tries to settle herself against the forthcoming storm. Her heels click and slither on the stone floor as she alters her stance slightly. She tries to focus on the view outside and ignore the hammering of her heart in the face of taking a thrillingly unpredictable beating.

There is no warning. The lash is just suddenly there, thudding down across her upper back, the tip searing into the side of her already pulsing breast. She hadn't expected it there and momentarily she chokes for breath, before she has regained a steady rhythm of breathing, the lash is back. This time the master has moved and is standing almost beside her so that it falls with even greater force as his arm follows through the stroke in a full blooded throw. It cracks across her buttocks and this time the tip digs agonisingly into the front of her pelvis, just above her groin. She is helpless to stop herself bringing one leg up instinctively and twisting away from the spiteful impact. This makes her spin at the end of her chain and as she does she catches a glimpse of the master. He is still smiling and is drawing the lash back for the next stroke. Sarah knows he will deliver it somewhere that will make her squirm and spin and hop. That is how he wants her; dancing to his tune. She feels the hot wetness inside her; she wants him. She is desperate to know how big and hard his cock is and what it will feel like when at last he deigns to put it into one of her holes. The third lash is delivered as she is trying to settle again. This time he curls the leather around the upper part of one thigh so that the lash wraps itself at dizzying speed and delivers a blinding flash of agony right below her passionately engorged labia. She hops and twirls at the end of the chain, ungainly, naked and vulnerable. But proud of how much skill the master is investing in this beating. She will treasure the marks from it, whatever the men decide about her future. She knows a real artist is at work on the canvas of her helpless body.

By the time she hears her current master enter, she is wrecked. Sweat streams from her exhausted body, her head hangs between her shoulders and all she can do is watch beads of sweat drip from her nipples and from her rat-tailed hair as the whip continues to land. Ecstasy explodes within her, detonated when the new master stops and feels her cunt and her breasts. Now the beating is over, she has taken her ten extra. There is a pause. Her current master moves behind her to join the new one. There is the rustling of cloth and then heaven!

The new master is naked. He stands close behind her and reaches around to fondle her seething breasts again and she can feel the iron hard length of cock between her buttocks.

Suddenly ashamed of her slovenly stance she raises her head and tries to swing her pelvis and grind backwards onto the cock. There is laughter behind her.

But then the new master is in front of her, strong hands lift her thighs and with a sigh of gratitude she wraps her legs around him and sinks down onto the wonderful, thick shaft of cock that slides into her so easily in the wake of her beating. Immediately she starts trying to grip the phallus inside her at the same time as she starts using her chained wrists to haul herself up by. Slowly and sensually she grinds and writhes on her new master's shaft. Greatly daring she bends her head forwards and rests her face on his neck, inhaling the smell of aftershave, body lotion and fresh sweat. She sighs again as she feels him twitch inside her, it spurs her on to make greater efforts to lift herself and then sink slowly back down his divine length. Her stomach muscles begin to cramp both from effort and approaching orgasm. Fingernails are suddenly driven hard into the whipped flesh of her buttocks as the master begins to move inside her. She throws her head back just as the man behind her swings the heavy flogger in across her already flogged shoulders.

She is launched helplessly into a frenzy of bouncing up and down on the impaling cock and a wild jerking of her upper body as the whip clubs and stings her. Her climax is so devastating she never feels the master spend inside her, she is only aware of being left hanging limply in her chains while her wrists are freed and then she slumps onto all fours. The new master clicks his fingers and slowly, semen leaking down her thighs, sweat stinging in her welts, Sarah goes to him.

On the way back to the house she whimpers her need for a toilet and is allowed to half crouch, thighs wide spread in a flower bed. There she urinates while the men look on.

They resume their seats on the terrace and she is allowed to stretch out on the cool grass before them.

She lies on her back, letting the grass cool her blistered skin. Through half closed eyes she watches the summer sky and feels the warmth of the sun on her face. Vaguely she hears male voices discussing the loudness of her orgasms, how quickly she can be induced to orgasm a second time, how long she can stand hot waxing between her legs. On and on it goes. She smiles, a hot warmth melting her stomach once more as she relaxes in the knowledge that whatever the men are talking about, it is nothing that need concern her mentally. Her body is all they require from a slave.

As the sun begins to set and the air cools, the men stand and she crawls indoors after them. They take her to the playroom and subject her to an hour in the breast press.

She is shaking and sweating, face down across a leather bench, her squashed breasts and clamped nipples are pounding out a symphony of thudding pain and sharp agony beneath her when a sale agreement is put on the leather in front of her and both men sign it. Through heavy lidded eyes she watches the strong fingers of both men make the marks on the paper. There is no name on it for her, she is simply 'slave'. The deal is struck and then sealed by both men coming in her mouth, one after the other; the semen of the old and the new mingling in her throat and on her face, symbolising perfectly the continuance of her slavery and the smooth transition from one master to another.

Two weeks later she is standing in the hall, hitching up her pencil skirt and checking the seams on her stockings are straight. She is dressed according to the new master's strict instructions, seamed stockings, high heeled court shoes, dark blue business suit and cream shirt. Beneath, she wears a bra, thong and suspenders. She feels over dressed but still harbours a hot softness at her belly from where Mcloud, as she can now think of him, bent her over the kitchen table a few minutes before and gave her a farewell fuck. He was on his way up to London to start looking for a new slave and was whistling happily as he left her frantically wiping herself between her legs before any of his sperm stained her clothes.

Her few possessions are stacked behind her in one suitcase and a trunk. Assured that her seams are straight she stands, calm and patient, waiting for the car her new master is sending. She hears gravel crunching under tyres; there is a knock at the door and she opens it. A powerfully built man in his mid thirties stands before her. He smiles and indicates the car. She follows and notices that it carries no taxi plates. The man holds one of the rear doors open for her and Sarah climbs in, making no attempt to keep her skirt down. She opens her legs widely to step into the car and shows her stocking tops to the nakedly lustful gaze of the driver. Sarah is experienced enough in the ways of masters to know how this will go. He is clearly a friend of her new owner and on the way to his house the car will pull onto a side road and park. The driver will come to the back door and open it. In coarse, brutal terms he will instruct her to open his trousers, take out his penis and suck it until he ejaculates. He will make sure that some of his spunk is spilled onto her face and into her hair. It will be done as coldly as possible, the man will make no move to enter the car; just stand beside it.

She will not be able to see anything of him apart from his rigid penis jutting arrogantly from his flies. All that will matter to all concerned is that her mouth will passionately signal, by its humble offering of its soft lips and tight little interior to the careless spurting of spunk from a total stranger, that she is quite prepared to accept her new master's complete authority over her body and to whom it is offered.

When she arrives at her new home the new master will smell and see her state as she will have been forbidden to attempt any cleaning and the driver will have watched her in the mirror.

The subsequent beating – her first in her new home will be bitterly hard and will set the pattern for all future whippings. She sighs in resignation at her own masochism as she registers the happy tingle of warmth that spreads through her at the thought of the coming cruelty.

But then she is just a slave.

She hears footsteps on the gravel and sees the man carrying her trunk out. It has her initial and name on its lid. She smiles as she watches it go by the window. Her new master will laugh when he sees it. Sarah Lave. S.Lave. Slave.

It is her name, her function, her calling, her profession. It is her self. Perfect.

Other books by Sean;

Church of Chains

Taming the Brat

Tales from the Lodge (with Falconer Bridges)

The Story of Emma

The Modern Arena series of novels have acquired one of the most dedicated followings of any Silver Moon saga.

Into the Arena

The Gladiator

The Prize

Slave's Honour

Last Slave Standing

Pain ordained

by Richard Garwood

Now here's a newcomer. Richard has a lot of fresh ideas and we'll hear more from him in the coming months.

How ever had I got here? It was dark and it was chilly. Something seemed to have happened to me and although I could feel my hands and feet I couldn't move them. I had no idea where I was. I was shivering. Was it fear or chill? I tried to collect my ideas. Neither my brain nor my body were working. Perhaps I was dead. I felt a lump in my throat and recognised it as the beginnings of panic. I called out, but there was no response except a hollow echo. I felt a gathering pressure in my bladder and knew that if I was frightened any further I would pee myself and soak my clothes. My clothes. I realised that I could feel no touch of cloth against my skin. I pulled at my left wrist. Something soft but very strong held me. I curled my fingers to my wrist and felt the texture of thick fur. Embedded in it was something which was holding my wrist at the full extent of my arm. I tried my right wrist. The reaction was just the same. I tried again to move my feet but my ankles were held in a grip which meant that I was unable to move my legs.

I checked out my body to see if I was injured. I was sure I was naked. I knew that I was lying on my back, spread-eagled. I could feel the pressure on my shoulder blades and my buttocks and against my calves and heels. None of this was painful, but I had no control over anything, body or mind. I was beginning to lose control of my emotions as fear stalked through the empty wasteland of my mind. I tried a prayer, but my situation was such that I could not concentrate on the object of my prayer, and in any case I felt that I probably wasn't worthy to present a prayer, as I had got myself into this situation. I suppose that it was entirely wrong of me to have gone out on Saturday evening for a drink in a club on the other side of town. I should have kept my eye on my drink when I was approached by the best looking man in the club who offered me compliments. He was perfectly civilised but I wasn't used to this sort of flattery and I didn't realise that he had spiked my drink until I started to find my voice slurring and my legs wouldn't work.

I closed my eyes in the dark, letting the alpha waves take over so that they might return me to some rational state. I concentrated on trying to look down on my body from a point about one and a half metres above my navel. I concentrated hard. What I needed to know was what I looked like and whether that was a clue to my present position.

The only sound I could hear was the blood pounding in my ears. With an effort of will which temporarily dispelled the fear I began to summon up an image of myself. I began at my feet. They were carefully tended feet with no blemishes. They were narrow and size three in British sizes. I tried to remember the USA and European equivalents, but found that I couldn't. It was irrelevant. I moved to my ankles which were slender and graceful, likewise my shins and calves. I was brought up short because I knew that what I was seeing was my captive naked body. Panic began to stir again as I wondered what had become of my favourite high heeled sandals, the long floating skirt and the silk shirt which was so soft and smooth against my skin and whose pleats concealed the size of my breasts and the erect nipples which crowned them. I had a single Debit card in the side pocket of my skirt, a couple of folded tissues and four ten pound notes. My house key and car key were on a chain attached to my leather belt and wedged at the bottom of my right hand pocket. Nothing else, no make-up, no tampon, no comb or brush, no coat. Nothing.

In my mind's eye I visualised my thighs. Like my calves they were slender and without any signs of fat or dimpling. They were lightly tanned like the rest of my skin. I concentrated harder and saw my thighs meet and the naked mound and the slot of my vulva still closed despite my spread legs. I loved myself between my thighs. This complex and wonderful device with its little bud which had no other function than to give me sexual pleasure. How good it had been at that, and with so little effort. My belly was flat with the navel vertically elongated, neatly contained within the strong arc of my hips. Immediately above my hips my waist shrank in to a circumference of no more than fifty-one centimetres. My chest always appeared to me to be exceptionally bony, This was because my ribs, like the ends of my hip bones, showed through the skin.

I suddenly remembered weight lifting in front of a mirror and seeing the muscles on my belly contracting and the arch formed by my lowest ribs looking like the supporting roof arches in a Gothic cathedral. I loved to stroke my belly and feel the bony arch through my skin. I loved looking at it and having it admired by the very few who had ever been privileged to see it. I moved on to my breasts and gazed at them with the adoration which they seemed to inspire in others. Their spread, where they were attached to my chest, took up the whole breadth of my front elevation, but what had always been so remarkable was that from the time they grew to their full size they were conical, and they didn't disappear onto my chest when I lay down. They were both solid and firm. I enjoyed the sight of my nipples sitting in the midst of the areola, always prominent but much more so when I was aroused, and I used to thank God that I did arouse without a lot of hesitation.

I could readily see my collar bones which always looked frail but were quite strong enough for anything that I had ever wanted to do. I could make deep hollows in the top of my chest by bringing my shoulders forward. Thinking about it, I realised that I have quite wide shoulders and slender arms and neck. The muscles in my arms are visible when I flex them, but I have never looked like a body builder, rather just toned.

For some reason I found it very difficult to visualise my face, but I knew I had small ears, thick auburn hair, green eyes and very good teeth.

That was it, then. What could I do next, I wondered. The decision making was taken away from me as an increasingly bright but strangely flickering light reached my eyes and some none too musical chanting accompanied it. As the light increased I realised that I was secured on a platform about seventy-five centimetres above the floor. I could move my head enough to see that I was held by cuffs at ankles and wrists and that I was quite naked. Slowly marching figures entered the room in which I lay. They were hooded and their outer garments looked like those of monks I had seen in monasteries. Each of them had a staff with a lighted candle at the top end, held above the head. This cast an excellent light on me, but left their faces in shadow. They formed a circle round the platform. I was relieved to see that they carried no tools or weapons with which to hurt me.

They took up position round where I was lying and each one pushed his staff into a socket in the floor just behind him. The person immediately behind me launched into a speech, but it was intoned with great speed and was delivered in a monotone with no stress on words for added meaning. It seemed to be in a language which I vaguely recognised, but I managed to pick up only a few words which I thought were familiar, but the whole was incomprehensible to me. After a while I tuned into the speech and picked up that it was in English but with many foreign names.

"Oh Adonai, Oh Beelzebub, Oh Master of the hidden universe," was repeated at regular intervals by all those present. I realised that this was a religious service, I feared that I might be the sacrifice. I tried to shout at them over the sound of their voices, but a figure beside me put a large hand over my mouth and pressed my head down so that it was jammed hard against the table beneath me. Table, I didn't think so. This was an altar. I could just make out the figure standing at the far end of it where my feet were tied down. I thought that what he was doing was supernatural as he stepped forward and stood between my legs, but I quickly realised that the altar that I lay on was shaped so that my trunk and head were on the main part and my arms and legs were on extensions which were attached to the body of the altar.

He stood between my pinioned thighs as the chant became faster and more threatening. He kicked what I took to be a bucket on the floor in front of him. The speaker behind me went silent and the group descended from the chant into a tuneless, wordless humming. He reached forward and took my head in his hands, the ends of his fingers pressing quite gently against my throat. The big hand was withdrawn from my mouth and I inhaled a good lungful of air so that I could shout or scream. As I did so I felt the fingers press harder against my throat and I exhaled slowly and quietly, trying to relax whilst I began to be consumed by desperate fear. Another of the group had produced a bundle of incense sticks and was lighting them at a candle, he must have inserted them in some sort of holder just behind and to the side of my head. Thick smoke drifted across my face and I breathed in some unrecognisable perfume which I thought might choke me but its effect was to make me feel slightly drowsy, a welcome, but worrying change. Still, if I could do nothing to protect myself, I might as well be relaxed rather than terrified.

I hadn't noticed the figure at the end of the altar bend forward with something gleaming in his hand. This was passed to the hand which was over my mouth and suddenly I felt something pushed between my lips and my jaws were forced apart so that it penetrated into mouth between my teeth. I tried moving my head, but strong hands held it still. I could see the figure on my left raise something in his hands to a general acclamation. He brought it down beyond my sight line and then pressed it to the top of what I realised was a funnel in my mouth. Liquid began to trickle down the funnel and I swallowed it as fast as I could. I recognised the strong fruity taste of a not very good red wine as it hit the back of my throat. I began to choke and cough and the pouring stopped and the funnel was lifted an inch in my mouth. I recovered and the alcohol continued to trickle down into my stomach. I began to pant with the exertion of swallowing whilst lying down and breathing when my mouth was full of the funnel and the wine. Bending over me I could see the glittering eyes of the holder of the funnel and the bottle. They were watching me, but it was not my face they were observing with such callousness, but my breasts rising and juddering as I gulped for air and my chest expanded to draw in more oxygen.

At last the pouring stopped and the funnel was removed. I gulped and coughed but it was over in a minute. The chanting had begun again, the voices seemed more urgent this time and the invocation louder. My head was spinning and I felt what little strength I had in my limbs dissipate. Another of the group had produced a bottle and I dreaded that he was going to pour more alcohol into me, but this time it seemed that the red wine was to be wasted as he poured a thin trickle over my face, down my neck, over both breasts and then he paused at my navel as I sucked in my breath and he filled the concave of my belly. I felt the trickle between my thighs and then realised that he was pressing the slender neck of the bottle against my lips and as they parted, into my vagina. Wine gushed into me and then out again and the sensation of being filled and emptied and the sound of the liquid and the pressure against my bladder made me pee myself despite my efforts not to. I heard the splash of the wine and my pee in the bucket beneath me. I felt ashamed that I had let myself go.

The gushing ended and the figure directly in front of me produced another bottle and washed me clean with the wine. I was becoming light headed and tried to cling to reality as best I could. The hands holding my head tipped it forward so that I could see the length of my body and the dark figure standing, unmoving between my legs. The chant continued and I tried to prevent it from entering my consciousness by repeating the Lord's prayer and then I attempted the Creed, but ended with Hail Mary, full of grace. My attempts at bringing to bear the traditional Anglican Christian prayers and the catalogue of beliefs was futile. Sadly it didn't even comfort me, let alone deter my tormentors. The foreboding figure's hands began to undo the rope sash which bound his clothes at the waist. I watched in disbelieving fascination as he wound one end of the rope round his fist and then raised his arm above his head and brought down the rope across my belly. It stung me. How it stung me. I felt the breath go out of my lungs as the rope bit me and the clawing traceries of pain spread across from hip to hip. I wanted to cry out, but all my breath was busy trying to regulate the pain. I wanted to move my body to reduce the agony, but I could writhe only a few centimetres and turning to left or right was almost impossible. As the pain started to ease I cried out "No, no, no!" but the chant continued and a second slash from the rope caught me from my cunt to my navel and up to the lowest ribs. This time I gasped and screamed at the same time, begging for mercy. But there was no mercy. I felt the pain between my legs as if I had been scalded and it spread in a solid band of agony up my belly cutting its path across my white skin until it culminated in a vicious graze of the skin stretched tightly over my ribs. I screamed and choked and implored. I felt pressure in my throat and roaring in my ears. I didn't think I could stand many more of these applications of the rope. In my agony I had failed to notice that the people on either side of me had unknotted their belts from their waists and were adapting them as whips in the same way as my first assailant had done.

The chant changed to a regular and well spaced repetition of the names. At the end of the second cycle I saw the figure at the end of the altar raise his arm again and he brought the rope down along the right side of my belly just inside my hip bone and up onto my ribs. I screamed again and as far as I was able I moved in my bonds to try to get the blood flow going to carry away the pain which for a moment quite engulfed me. At the second name being spoken, the man next but one to my head on my right cut me across the top of my thighs with his rope. I could manage no more than a guttural grating cry. Tears had begun to well up in my eyes and were coursing down my cheeks into my hair.

The next slash was to my breasts and I saw the rope compress them and then they sprang back into their usual shape, but now there was a developing weal across them and I wept the faster, not only because of the pain but because of the assault on my beautiful breasts which up to that point had been a source of only joy and pleasure. The striking moved to my left side and a rope caught me a cutting blow just below my breasts on the skin stretched tight across my ribs. I howled the cry of the despairing doomed, but could not find the strength to move. There was a long pause before the next name and then a cut over my right hip bone and across my belly with the end of the rope catching my navel and driving out all the air in my chest. I gasped to bring air back so that I could breathe more regularly and cry out against my torment, but I had hardly done so when the figure at the end of the altar touched me between my thighs and opened my labia. Despite the intrusion into my body, this at least was not as painful as the previous cuts had been. It took me several seconds to realise that the fingers that had opened me were now expertly manipulating my clitoris. I fought the symptoms of arousal, which despite the discomfort of lying on the altar, to say nothing of the whipping I had received, were beginning to be evident, at least to me. It was not long before the massage and its pressure brought the response which always came to me as I enjoyed my fingers pressed into me between my legs, and I began to drip from my vagina the juices which made penetration all so much easier and my pleasure so much greater. I determined to deliver myself up to the pleasure which I was receiving, but suddenly, as I lay with my mouth open and my eyes closed, it ceased and before I could utter a protest a blinding pain caught my cunt. It was impossible for me to locate exactly where it started or what had caused it, but the agony was so intense that I could not bring myself to cry out and my thoughts were all concentrated on the terror of any repetition of the excruciating sensation. It seemed to take several minutes for the pain to abate. As I opened my eyes it was to see the figure to my right raise his rope and slash it down again between my thighs.

I kept drawing breaths into my lungs as if I was trying to fill them to bursting point. I could hear myself crying "Oh, oh, oh, oh," as waves of agony swept over me from my tortured clitoris. It was pain such as no one deserved to suffer. So sharp was the intensity of the agonising cut to my cunt that I thought I must be bleeding and likely to bleed to death. My throat was constricted and the roar in my ears grew louder. I was aware only that I had been savagely assaulted in that part of me that was given to me entirely for my own pleasure and now it was the source of such an extremity of pain that I would have wished it away as the source of agony. The members of the group seemed keen on ensuring that I had the maximum of agony from each blow I received. I felt the hands which had held my head replaced by others. There was movement around the altar and people seemed to be changing places.

Within a few moments there was a shout from the leader of the group and the others began to say the names again. There was a pause and then the whipping began again, this time much faster, so that I had no chance to recover from one strike before another, aimed at a different part of my body simply increased the distress inflicted on me. Despite the ferocity of the torment, I was able to consider the damage which the assault from these whips was doing to me. I suspected that it was more searing than penetrating, but that the pain itself might seriously affect me.

In that diagnosis I seemed to be nearly right. I felt consciousness slipping away from me. The ropes descended on my body, biting into my belly, cutting into my cunt, piercing my labia and abrading my clitoris, pushing my breasts into unnatural and throbbing shapes and yet the agony was diminishing to a state where I was able to carry the pain which they were inflicting. At first I was pleased to be able to praise God for at least this part of my deliverance, but then I remembered the work of pain controlling endorphins, which for a while prevented the worst agonies from overwhelming the sufferer. So this release was down to me. But who was I down to? Perhaps I ought to be thanking God after all.

In the candlelight I looked down at my suffering body, seeing a rope brought down from above its wielder's shoulder height, and cutting mercilessly into my flesh. Even in the subdued light I could see angry patches growing at the cross over points of the stripes. My body was bathed in sweat which ran from my scalp into my eyes. I felt myself to be horribly abused and anguished, but I felt so ashamed that I had given even the slightest sign of pleasure when I was handled and that the hand working on my clitoris had made the whipping no less painful but associated with my pleasure. I was amazed at myself for wanting to be whipped more and more. Perhaps I saw myself as a martyr to these tormenting demons. In which case I was a martyr displayed most openly and erotically. This in itself was enough to make me wonder about myself and my desire, hitherto, to be pure and set an example.

My thoughts occupied a very few seconds. I came back to the immediate situation and found myself writhing on the altar, tilting my hips from side to side and leaving my open cunt for everyone to see. The chant broke off. I felt the tears on the side of my face and I gasped for air to fill my lungs and call up more hormones to relieve my agony. In the midst of my self-regarding thoughts I felt a hand grasp my right breast. Fingers curved round it and found the weals and touched them gently. Another hand took hold of my left breast and having traced the visible signs of my torment, the fingers concentrated on my nipple, in which exploration it was joined by the other hand. I was shamed that my body could react to these anonymous pressures by engorging my breasts and bringing my nipples erect. I should have been filled with distaste and loathing at their touch, but my need to be comforted and pleasured was greater than my revulsion at their manipulation of my tortured breasts. The hands stayed where they were, but two hooded heads closed off my line of sight and two sets of lips and teeth enclosed my nipples, sucking and nibbling whilst the hands palpated each of my breasts. It was done with supreme confidence and an evident knowledge of the effect that it was having on me.

Beyond the heads I could see nothing, but whilst it was possible to enjoy what was being done to me, I was appalled when another head bent towards mine and lips pressed against mine and I allowed a thick long tongue into my mouth. I wanted to bite this invader, but the flickering tongue sought out my own and involved itself with mine, sliding against it and exchanging juices in the most intimate of ways. I felt the tongue move against my lips and then my teeth, my whole being and all of my attention was taken up with the suckling of my breasts and the tongue gesticulating in my mouth. This is probably why I was utterly unprepared for the sudden pressure at the gates of my sex. It was not fierce, but something was being rubbed up and down between my labia and on to my clitoris. I feared I was already more than moist between my thighs, but I did not expect to be suddenly impaled by something driven deep into my vagina. I could not tell what this might be, but it was long and it was thick, and then I felt the whiskery impact of the pubic hair and the man's thighs against the inner faces of mine. He sank deep into me and my attention transferred to what was happening inside me. I could feel him lean back from me and slowly withdraw himself from me, only to return with increased pressure and begin a pumping movement which struck at the neck of my womb. I felt his fingers spread across my belly and his thumb against my clitoris. He moved his thumb up and down as he pushed in and pulled out of me. I knew I was being raped, but this was no furtive, momentary, brutal shafting accompanied by threats and ineptitude. This was something done to please both of us, despite my inability to participate except as a victim.

I didn't count the number of thrusts, but I felt his priapic ardour increasing and the speed increased until above all the other sounds in my ears and the violations elsewhere of my body, I heard a shout of triumph and I felt him jerk himself out of me and spray his jism over my thighs and belly. I tried to hate him for what he had just done to me, but there was no individual to hate, just as there were none to forgive. His place was at once taken by another. I felt him pull up the rough cassock which enveloped him and I felt the tip of his cock push straight into me followed by the shaft. This one was not as long a the first one, so that it was our pubic bones which ground together, rather than striking at my cervix. However, this was a thicker implement and it seemed to fill my cunt with its bulk. He made no attempt to pleasure me but thrust each time as far as he was able and then withdrew for a further thrust. I tried closing my vaginal muscles on this solid tool, but its owner was as substantial as it was and he pulled and pushed for what seemed to be several minutes before he, in his turn, tore himself out of me and drenched my thighs in his sticky come.

I was fearful that I should have to endure all these unknown men's attentions, but the next two made no attempt to penetrate me with their cocks, but they spread my juices on their fingers and pulling my buttocks apart they put their fingers in my anus. I screamed and tried to pull away from their incursions, but I was amazed to find that both of these invaders were jerking their hands on their cocks and suddenly spraying me with their jism. Perhaps I now looked too disgusting for them to penetrate me. The mouth on mine was removed and I was able to breathe more easily. The mouths on my breasts ceased their work and the heads of all three disappeared from my view. I was now able to register very clearly the figure now pressing his cock into me, but he seemed to be a shadow in a shadow, until he leaned towards me and grasped my hips with his big hands, using his grip to lever himself into me. Once in he stayed just where he was so I forced down on my pelvic floor muscles in an effort to expel him, but all I achieved was a harder grip on his cock which I could feel pulsing inside me. Imperceptibly he began to withdraw, but I maintained my grip and after a few moments he reversed his motion and began to thrust in again. I had had little experience of the delights of sex, but this was an entirely new approach for me and I relaxed my grip and let him proceed, given that I had no alternative. The pulsing, quivering cock was slowly pressed into me and then he began a series of tiny movements sending sparks of energy into me until, without warning he pulled right out of me and in an instant there was a fountain covering my belly and thighs.

It had been difficult for me to work out just how many men were in the group. As another one came to take his pleasure of my body other hands were caressing my breasts and rotating my nipples backwards and forwards. These hands were quite gentle, or was it, I wondered, in comparison with the thrashing I had received and the power of the invading cocks. I could feel my body aching and some patches of biting pain where the whips had found some delicate tissue, or an especially heavy blow had cut into me. Now, as this last ravisher finished with me and was not immediately replaced, I began to wonder what my future was, always supposing that I had any at all. The thought frightened me almost to the point of preventing me from a rational reflection of ideas. They had drugged me and abducted me. They had stripped off my clothes and manacled my arms and legs to some outlandish table, which I still thought of as an obscene altar. They had chanted some hideous rite over me whilst thrashing me without mercy. Now they had handled my breasts, invaded my mouth and had gang raped me. What, I wondered was there left for them to do, other than kill me and dispose of my body. At once

I was less afraid and more resigned to the ending of my life. I began a silent confession of my sins and offered a prayer for the safety of my soul.

In the midst of my attempt to make my passage into the hereafter more saintly, I felt fingers at my wrists and ankles and the straps which held me being undone. My arms were stiff with being kept in one position for so long and powerful hands were massaging them to restore the proper circulation of the blood and ease the muscles. To my surprise I was being lifted from the altar and was being held on either side to help me stand on my feet. To my distress mingled juices splashed from my vagina on to my feet and I must have seemed a forlorn and dishevelled figure with my body covered in smarting weals, my cunt dripping and my legs hardly able to support me.

They walked me across the room which was becoming increasingly dark as the candles guttered out one by one. As we approached the wall my hands were seized and held in front of me, whilst a pair of hand cuffs were attached to my wrists. A smooth running chain hauled the cuffs into the air until I was standing, virtually on tiptoe, surrounded by the group of men. One of them stepped forward and ran his hands over my shoulders. He enclosed my breasts in his hands as far as he was able and he pressed my nipples with his thumbs. He almost encircled my waist with his hands and then grasped a buttock in each hand, pressing and squeezing the globes. A finger sought out my anus and I shifted my feet to avoid his penetration. Almost immediately he had reached between my thighs and had begun to rub my clitoris with his fingers. I began to move my feet up and down, which made my bottom and my breasts jiggle. I was conscious of the eyes of the group focused on my naked body, but I was beyond shame. The manipulation of my clitoris was expert, if strangely distant. I could not see my assailant's face but he was touching me with considerable knowledge and skill in the most tender and secret parts of my body. I could think of nothing I could do to resist this attention, but worse than that I didn't think that I wanted to resist it. I realised that I was getting out of control in a way that I had managed to avoid so far. My head was pounding, dew was gathering at my cunt lips and there was that sharp fluttering in my belly which meant that I was about to put all other considerations on one side as I concentrated on my orgasm.

The dew began to drip and I closed my eyes as bright lights seemed to flash in my head and I began to buck my hips to get faster penetration from the fingers and bring myself to an orgasm. I wondered how I could do this after I had been so dreadfully abused, and worse, how I could not be paralysed by shame in the display of my naked body in the throes of ecstasy. I at once dismissed the thoughts and concentrated on my spinning head and my fiery cunt, with the passion pulses pushing up my belly and my nipples standing out on my breasts to leave no one in doubt about the state of my arousal. I knew I was about to crown it all for myself when I felt a savage blow across my shoulders and another across my buttocks. Someone was thrashing me again at the point when my life should have been consumed in a single flare of the fieriest passion. I found I could ignore the slashes and I concentrated with all my will on the reward I had planned for myself as a farewell to the life I had known. And then, almost out of nowhere, there it was, a paroxysm of the most powerful, muscle contracting, breath annihilating, eyes flaring, mouth screaming orgasm that it was possible to have. At its height a calm came upon my thoughts and I knew that no one could ever take this away from me, and at least I had experienced the ultimate.

My head reeled as I began to come down from the height I had so unexpectedly attained. As my orgasm tailed off the beating declined in intensity and at last I was left dangling from the chain with my body arched outwards and my head thrown back between my arms. The chain was slowly descending and my knees buckled beneath me. I began to collapse on the floor as I was lowered from my dangling position and I ended lying across the boots of one of the group as another one undid my handcuffs which were whisked away above me. I felt a sudden flash in my face but I was blinded by the light and was quite unable to locate its source. Most important was that I knew that I was free of all constraints for the first time since I became aware of the horror I found myself in. Sadly the freedom was useless to me as I was not in control of my body.

The owner of the boots extricated them from under me and the group moved away. I lay on the carpeted floor on my left side with my left arm thrust out beyond my head, which was using it as a cushion. My right arm was lying behind me so that my front was unobscured from the sight of any one who wanted to see more of it. My legs were apart and slightly drawn up towards my chest but I recognised that what light there was would show my naked labia, quite possibly slightly open. All that mattered to me was that I should regain my strength, and lying relatively comfortably might make that possible. I was aware of the group on the far side of the room discussing me in whispers. A sentence from one of them seemed to be associated with a turn of the heads in my direction. I was well beyond caring what they were deciding. Nothing could be more painful, or exhausting than what I had already endured. It was a pity that I was not better at predicting the future.

I shifted my position to ease my battered body, but I needed to keep my legs apart because of the bruising between my thighs. It wasn't a graceful or dignified position, letting the cool air penetrate me, but at least it was more comfortable than the alternatives. I could feel some return of my strength and I began to pray for my release and prepare my mind for whatever the future held. Surely they were sated with their torture of my body and the degradation of my spirit. They had achieved some sort of sexual satisfaction, both in whipping me and in piercing my body with their cocks. What more could they desire of me. They knew that I could never recognise them again and that I had no idea where I was, so they, at least were safe. Even their DNA was so mixed both on and in me that it would be impossible to identify them by the usual scientific means.

At all times one or other of my tormentors kept an eye on me, so that any attempt to make a dash for the corridor by which they had entered would be useless. At last the group moved towards me and one of them told me to stand up, which I struggled to do at once. I stood before them with the evidence of their brutality vivid on every part of my body. I adopted the classic protective pose with my right hand covering my crotch, and my left forearm parallel to the ground covering my left breast and holding my right breast in my hand, or as much of it as I could hide from their greedy eyes.

I was told that they thought that I needed some exercise after all the lying about which I had enjoyed and that they were going to see if I was good at running. They had decided on a pursuit race round the room with first one and then another of the group taking over the pursuit as I passed the altar which had been pushed across the corridor opening. We were to run counter clockwise starting by the altar, where I was to have a three metre lead. I began to ask what the outcome might be if I drew away from them or if they caught up with me, but I could get no sense out of them. I stretched myself and particularly my legs before we started and watched carefully the starter's arm.

I was away as soon as it started its downward movement and at once managed to extend the lead on my pursuer by two long strides. Apart from my breasts, which were bouncing at every step, I carry no surplus weight and I have managed to keep quite fit. My pursuer was handicapped by his robes. My hair streamed behind me and I began to increase my lead. By the end of the first lap of this quite substantial room I had gained five metres on my pursuer who handed over at the starting point to one of his friends who was apparently fitter and faster than his predecessor. Even so I did not much fear that he would catch me on his lap and I hoped that I would be able to outrun the next pursuer. It was a near thing, and had this runner come after me on the first lap he would have caught me. As it was he came close, but even at the end he was unable to touch me.

The third runner seemed to make a poor start but very soon strode fast behind me. I began to feel that crawling sensation on my back which comes with being chased and the fear of being caught. Fear began to develop in my belly and I stumbled for a moment when I came to a corner of the room. Fear drove me forward again and I increased the speed and length of my stride, though I was beginning to get a bit out of breath and sweat was beginning to run down my body and out of my hair and into my eyes. At the next corner I looked back to see that I had gained a metre on my pursuer, but that he was coming on strongly and steadily. Because I am so light I found it easier than the heavier men to make the turns and my initial acceleration was better than theirs. On the straights they made up ground, but still I was outrunning them, though I had no idea how long I could keep it up, especially as I had to hold my breasts in my hands so that they did not slow me down. This wasn't good for my cornering and was one of the main reasons that they were beginning to gain on me.

The fourth runner appeared to be carrying a small baton in his hand and he ran faster than any of the others. He began to gain on me at once and even the fear of capture did nothing for my speed. I began to panic. I excluded everything from my consciousness except the way ahead of me, my fear giving me tunnel vision to aid in my escape. My insides were churning and the emotion and the fierce activity were making my vagina drip onto my thighs. The feeling of gasping for breath, the fear of my unknown fate if I was caught and the now struggling physical activity brought forward the panic which had so far sustained my efforts, but was now beginning to slow me down, even though I was putting all my effort into running away. I had no time to wonder why I was running, after all the end would be the same whether I ran or crouched down in abject surrender.

I began to long for the opportunity to give up and take whatever punishment it brought me. I was gulping air through my mouth and my legs had begun to feel painful and not in total control. I could hear the slap of my pursuer's shoes on the floor and even above my own stertorous breathing, his deep intakes of breath. We were more than half way round the room when I became aware that he was very close behind me. I glanced over my shoulder to see his large figure, clothes streaming behind him, bearing down on me relentlessly. It was a dreadful mistake to look back. I was almost at the next left turn and I missed it and tangled my legs landing in an unceremonious heap which my pursuer fell over and landed on his chest with his arms spread out as if he was swimming. If I had had any sense I would have scrambled to my feet at once and I'd have left him behind sufficiently far for me to just about outrun the remaining two of them. Hindsight has twenty/twenty vision but all I knew was that I wanted to rest on the carpet and get my breath back. He gathered himself up and came back to me. I looked up into the shadowed place where only his eyes showed and for a moment I convinced myself that his irises were oblongs. Perhaps he was a demon after all.

He commanded me to get up and I lay still. He brought his hand out in front of him with the baton in it. He must have pressed a button because I felt a hideous jolt of electric current strike my left breast and a sense of being burnt and electrocuted at the same time. Every part of my body twitched and shook. My muscles contracted jerking my legs and flailing the air with my arms. The pain was excruciating and the scene around me went horrifyingly dim. There was a dreadful taste in my mouth and my belly contracted in a frightening spasm. I seemed to be leaking more from between my thighs as I clutched my cunt and my injured breast in my hands. I could hardly get my breath and I felt as if I was being strangled by an invisible ligature. My ears filled with the thunder of my beating heart which seemed to be at double its normal speed and much more violent. I gasped as if I was in the midst of an attack of asthma.

As the pain started to lessen I looked up to see the implacable eyes looking down at me and a voice asking if I wanted some more. It was as much as I could do to shake my head and I gathered my knees together and endeavoured to get myself up on all fours. As I did so I felt something shoved into my rectum and realised that he had stuck his baton into me. I had no doubt that its firing end was well inside me and I turned to pull it out, but I was thwarted by another of the hooded men who seized my hands and strapped them together. In my terror I knew that now I would have to out run them or a pursuer would catch up with me and press the hidden button and send me into unimaginable agony. Tears began to stream down my face and I shook from my distress at the prospect. Unless I ran.

I realised that I was very nearly in the classic sprint starting pose and before my tormentor could gather his wits I launched myself forward, despite the anguish I still felt in my body. He turned as I fled from him, but his start was clumsy and slow and I gathered all the strength I had to get away from him. I passed the starting place and saw a particularly large and apparently heavy figure waiting for his turn. This time I did not look back, but I fled from him as if from some murderous alien. The baton wagged between my buttocks, but I held my hands up to my breasts and pumped my legs for all I was worth. Curiously the short rest and the electric shock seemed to have given me more energy and strength than I could have believed I possessed. My fingers encountered the sore entry point of the spark which had disabled me. I was surprised that it was small and appeared to be superficial, though it stung as if I had been attacked by a hornet.

My fifth pursuer didn't seem to be gaining on me and out of the corner of my eye I saw him several metres behind me as I turned through the second corner. Nothing now would stop me escaping from the immolation of the baton piercing my buttocks. I ran on drawing breath through my mouth and with my legs and lungs screaming for relief, but I was totally dedicated to doing whatever I could to escape from this hideous agony. The last of the runners seemed to be less interested in the pursuit than the others, but half way round he managed a great spurt of speed and I sensed his approach. He was closing the gap between us as if I was hardly moving, and my breath was whistling in my throat and my legs felt like lead. It was only the worse alternative that spurred me on, but even then panic and terror were not enough to keep me going fast enough, compared with him.

I tried to fling myself forward as we approached the last few metres, but he was so close that his foot caught my ankle and I sprawled forward over the starting place. I lay unmoving with my arms stretched out in front of me awaiting my fate. I felt him get hold of the baton and at once I was suffused by a not totally unpleasant sensation. This must be low power, or the thing had virtually discharged itself when it hit me. Either way this was not what I expected or feared. I felt driblets of sweat run down my spine and collect in the small of my back. I had tried to protect my breasts as I fell, but the right one had gained an unpleasant carpet burn. Apart from that and the noise of my breathing and the pounding of my heart I appeared to have escaped the fate I thought awaited me.

A strong hand caught my wrists and pulled me to a kneeling position. The owner asked me if I thought that I was going to die and I nodded miserably. He asked me if I would now acknowledge the superiority of men in all things. I was so breathless that I could not answer him, even if I had wanted to and he stuck his fingers in my mouth and made me gag with the violence of the penetration. I heaved more air into my lungs as he removed his fingers and he asked me if I would worship at the essence of maleness. My gasping silence was apparently taken as acquiescence, if not agreement, and he unstrapped my wrists commanding me to stay kneeling.

There seemed to be some sort of discussion in progress within the group. My breathing and pulse returned to something like normal and I held my injured breasts in my hands as a comfort to them and to me. The group came towards me. One of them told me to keep quite still and to close my eyes. I sensed that one of the group was standing in front of me. He told me that I must do exactly what he commanded, neither more nor less and that if I did not I would receive another jolt which would make the last one feel like a flea bite. I shivered and hoped that I could follow his instructions.

In accordance with his wishes I reached my hands towards him and encountered a powerful, thick thigh. I moved my hands further up and found my fingers brushing against a distended scrotum, holding two eggs of massive size. I cupped these in my left hand and moved my right hand further up where I encountered a rigid cock of a size that meant that my fingers and thumb were unable to encircle it and of a length that meant that my hand could clasp only a small section of its monstrous length. I brought my head forward until my lips touched the tip of the helmet. I gave thanks that this was a clean and well washed penis and I touched the eye with my tongue, tasting it as slightly salty with a tinge of musk. I opened my jaws as far as I could to admit the thing into my mouth and it filled me between my teeth and began to press into the back of my throat whereupon I made a strangled cough. I continued to hold on to the shaft with my fingers, whilst keeping his testicles still with my other hand. I began to nod up and down, flickering my tongue round this monstrous thing and working at it with my lips and my fingers. This was my very first experience of oral sex and I realised that I lacked the capacity to do justice to such an organ.

I continued to work on the huge cock, but on his instruction I moved my hand from his scrotum and placed my fingers between my legs, though I could not bring myself to manipulate my tortured clitoris. I spread my knees and worked even faster at my task of stimulating its owner. I guessed that this was the one member of the group who had not penetrated my vagina earlier and I expected him to make me swallow his jism. I was right and in a few moments I felt his cock move in my hand and then the choking rush of jism shooting into my throat. I was quite unable to cope with the quantity he was producing which I feared would enter my windpipe, so I pulled my head back and received his ejaculation across my face, over my shoulders and down my breasts. I let go of him and was rewarded for my efforts by being told I would now have my reward for all my efforts. At their instruction I spread my knees further and reached back to hold my ankles with my hands. This was a pose so revealing and abandoned that I was voluntarily taking up, that I was amazed at myself.

A voice told me that I had worshipped at the shaft of virility and that I would now receive my reward for acknowledging that men were the natural masters of the world and of women in particular. I opened my mouth to disagree, but my reward came swift and terrible. I felt the touch of something between my open labia, giving my clitoris the most gentle of prods and then I knew what was to happen and I froze in dreadful fear, dripping terror juices from my vagina. I felt the first build up of the voltage as if a red hot glove had seized me between the legs and then there was nothing but agony and stars glowing white and red and my body contorted with exquisite and unbearable pain.

It must have been many hours later that I awoke from my pain-induced unconsciousness. Once again I was unable to move my limbs. I knew I was naked and that I smelled of wine; fruity red wine. I slowly opened my eyes to find that I began to recognise my surroundings. Above me was the great west window full of stained glass, to my right was the rest of the church, decorated for Easter. I realised with horror that I must be lying on the altar with my ankles and wrists tied to the stone embellishments. I was spreadeagled as if for some pagan ritual. I wept for the blasphemy of my position. it would have been better if they had done as I feared and killed me in their dungeon. I pulled at the ropes which bound me but I achieved nothing other than a tightening of the knots. I lay back sobbing. The time passed and I heard the familiar creak of the vestry door opening. I tried to cry out, but my voice had left me. The voices of the two churchwardens were talking about obscene photographs in the porch. One of them said she was glad the church itself had been left secure. I looked down the nave but could not see them until one of them came into view and screamed.

Mary ran towards the altar her face white and aghast. They threw a cassock over me and fumbled the ropes undone, lifting me off. Jean was already on her mobile asking emergency services to send the police and an ambulance. Mary had been cradling me in her maternal arms saying over and over again that it would be all right. She kissed me and said, "I'll take the service, you'll soon be all right, vicar."

Watch out for 'Painful Performance', his debut novel due out late in 2006

New Orleans — The Unseen Lord

By Syra Bond

Syra has already contributed two novels to Silver Moon and is working on her third currently.

"I crossed the Mississippi on the ferry from Algiers — the best bargain in town, free — and, as I sat in the broad, wire grill enclosed passenger deck with exploding fireworks filling the sky, I felt as if I was sailing into hell. It was New Year's Eve and in a less than reputable bar in the red light district that sprawls around Bourbon St — the noisy, brash ribbon of strip clubs, touts and prostitutes that lights up the French quarter of New Orleans — that frantic Creole city "that care forgot" — I met a young woman who told me a story so strange that, had I not witnessed it myself, I would have found unbelievable.

I saw her sitting with several men in a barely lit cubicle on the other side of the patchily lit bar. She was very attractive, striking and yet demure and, in the company of the men and with the noisy bustle of waiters and customers around her, she looked rather intimidated, even a little frightened. After a few minutes, I watched the men get up to leave. Each of them touched her in a strangely familiar way as they went, one stroking her cheek, another fondling her shapely breasts, one bending down and kissing her so hard on the mouth that it made her flinch and the last, the tallest of the group and the only white man, slipping his hand down the front of her white blouse and tightening his fingers around her left nipple so unyieldingly that, although she bore it, she narrowed her eyes to the narrowest slit as she withstood the pain in silence. They all stood around her for a few moments, the tallest, standing in front of her as she remained seated, drawing her face towards his bulging crotch with his hand then, acting in unison and not saying a word, they all left together. She, this fragile girl, nodded to each of them as they went, as if she was sealing some contract of which only she was aware. She watched the last one leave then turned to her empty glass and, with her dark eyes, stared into it as though it were an opening abyss. A waiter, older than the efforts of such a job easily tolerated, with a haughty look and tightly slicked back greying hair, brought her a fresh drink on a slopping wet tray. She did not acknowledge him but, rather theatrically, he bowed nevertheless, took a pace back, turned and left, bearing the still slopping tray on extended fingers high above his head.

I thought how sad and lonely she looked and, being alone myself and on the lookout for something interesting, I pushed my way through the crowded bar to join her.

"Your friends have left?" I said raising my eyebrows to see if she minded me sitting down.

"Mine?" she looked quizzical but nodded that I could sit beside her on the hard wooden bench of the cubicle. "My friends? No, I have never met them before," she said sipping her drink slowly.

Her thin white blouse, the top three buttons undone so that the shape of her firm breasts could easily be seen, was tucked neatly into a short black skirt. She had stockings on and, because one of her shapely legs was crossed over the other, I could see, beneath the tight-pulled material of the clinging skirt, the outline of the clasps of her suspenders pressing against her taut thigh. She wore plain black, high-heeled leather shoes one of which she dangled loosely on her toe.

"Oh," I said a little confused. "I imagined you knew them."

"No," she said wistfully as if acknowledging the fact was somehow a disappointment.

I called to the waiter and he brought two drinks without me ordering them. He placed them carefully on the table, bowed, stepped back and left.

I looked at this young woman, her pale, unblemished skin and her full lips spoke of youth but her practised certainty and dreamy eyes were the time-gained attributes of an older, more experienced woman. This mature air combined with her soft unaffected youthfulness were captivating. I asked where she was from and, as if I had turned a key in a lock, she started, in a soft, easy manner, talking about her life. Her name was Zandra, she was Portuguese but spoke only slightly accented and otherwise perfect English. Her father had been in the diplomatic service in Venezuela and because her parents were always at, or giving, parties for various foreign visitors she had been sent away to a private school until the age of eighteen.

"I went to a catholic convent run by nuns," she said, throwing back her head and laughing. "Corny I know but there are plenty of us you know, daughters of God." She smiled and sucked at the end of her forefinger for a moment. When she removed it her fingertip glistened with her spit. "That's where it all started, in that 'House of God'. The day I left there for good I found a note in my satchel. 'Go to the summerhouse and wait for me', she mouthed in a mock deep voice that lit up an undisguised childishness in her face as though her youthful simplicity had, for a moment, been set free. "I thought it was a joke," she continued, "a prank, there were lots of them going on during that last week or so of the final summer term."

"Did you have to wear a uniform?" I asked and felt embarrassed as soon as I had spoken. My question sounded so crass, so ridiculous. It was gratuitous, of course, she had opened up the fantasy of a beautiful virgin trapped with other girls in a finishing school and I wanted the whole picture. She did not judge my question and went straight to an answer.

"Of course," she replied first biting on then licking her well shaped, full and youthful lips. Biting them reddened them naturally and the swishing lick of the tip of her tongue covered them with a glistening gloss. "The skirt was always too short for comfort," she said looking down at her own short skirt and smiling. "I was always pulling at the hem. Always worrying about showing too much of my legs or worse! Too many prayers I suppose. Too much guilt. And habits die hard."

"What was it like having nuns to teach you?" I asked, listening to the inanity of my second question and blushing uncontrollably.

"Not bad. They were good teachers but they were also very strict. Just like the ones you read about! Frustrated and prim and keen on young girls' bottoms! They used to cane us if we did anything against their rules. On our bare bottoms. Can you imagine what it was like? Having to bend over and have your panties pulled down around your ankles. Just think of it. The exposure. I could feel my flesh squeezed tight between the insides of my thighs, I could feel its shape. You had to stay there, bent over like that, until they had finished with you. You weren't allowed to move until you were dismissed. They used to look at you for ages, rubbing their hands across your bottom before the caning began and afterwards they made you stay there for even longer until they decided you could go. They wanted to look at the red stripes they had made. They wanted to see how straight they were, how they stood out against the paleness of your bottom. They liked to touch them and see how much you flinched. 'You may pull your panties up and leave now,' they would say in the end and you were expected to bend over even more to do it. And if you flinched again when you pulled them up over your reddened bottom you could expect another helping. The prefects used to make us bend over in the prefects' room but they were not allowed to use a cane, they spanked us with a slipper or their hand. That was worse really. Some of those older girls did not stop at a spanking. Watching our buttocks reddening under their repeated blows was only a prelude to what they really wanted. And they got it, often as not, exactly what they wanted. Cows!"

"But the note," I said keenly, reminding myself of how she had begun her story. "What happened after you got the note?"

"Oh, the note. Yes, the note," she said wistfully as though thinking about her punishment in the convent had made her lose the thread of her story. As though the memory was both a horror and a delight, I could not tell which.

"Yes, 'Go to the summerhouse and wait for me'," I mimicked in the hope that my imitation would again release that naive simplicity I had seen before. But no, it had gone, perhaps lost forever or at least for the time being, locked away in some dark corner of her careworn mind.

"Of course. Well, I just went there," she continued, smoothing her hand across the top of her exposed thighs. "I sat on the circular seat in its centre and waited. It was one of those slatted seats you find built around big trees. It was a beautiful hot day and I stretched my legs out and there was no one around so I pulled my skirt up until I could see my underwear. It was as if I was daring myself to do something outrageous. A moment of release I suppose. After all those years of discipline I imagined being free, being able to do anything I wanted."

"What happened? Who came?" I asked thinking that she was going to tell me about her first liaison with a boy.

"No one came. But waiting there, doing what the note said, simply following the instruction had excited me. It was a weird feeling, I had never felt like it before."

"So nobody came," I said with undisguised impatience and missing the point she was making. "That was it."

"Well, not exactly. I lay back on the slatted wooden bench and rested my hands on the tops of my hips. The flat of my stomach dipped between them and beyond that was the creased-up edge of my skirt. I raised my hips slightly and the white of my panties came fully into view. The image struck me as if for the first time, that beautiful union of line, that delectable joining of material and flesh. It was different than being naked in the showers — and God, I'd seen enough of that — it was the excitement of the unseen, the exquisite delight of that which is merely hinted at. I knew what was beneath my panties but the fact that my panties covered it, the shape and contour of my flesh, was itself the excitement. The more I looked the more it thrilled me. The raised profile of my pubic bone pressing beneath the white cotton sent fluttering thrills through my stomach. The slight creases at the side as the material strained and the dipping slit that outlined the crevice of my flesh beneath made me tingle all over. The more I stared, the more I saw, the more I became excited. It flooded through me in waves. Thinking about it now still excites me just as much."

She looked down at the hem of her tight-pulled skirt and wriggled it a little higher. I saw the wedged-shaped delta of pale pink material that covered her flesh and I watched her squirm slightly against its pressure.

"I could not resist it," she continued. "And I let my fingers slide into the waistband of my panties. It was as if I crossed over into another zone of consciousness, like discovering a different world, every touch was a new sensation. I was electrified. I could feel every bit of the contact between my fingertips and my warm, wet flesh. Every pore seemed to fill me with a specific sensation. Every bead of sweat sent me its own message of joy. I remember it all so well, so precisely. I inhaled deeply, so deeply, and drew in the fresh fragrance of my wetness. I closed my eyes and let my head drop back. I felt the hairs at the base of my stomach, light, soft, easily parted, and then my trembling fingertips touched the upper part of my slit. It opened for me, welcoming, yearning. The parting of flesh that, when I made contact with it, opened like an oyster, revealing the wet inner petals, making them available, inviting me to slip my fingertips further along its sweet, moist valley. I raised my hips higher and touched the tip of my clitoris as it swelled to find my finger and I finished instantly, suddenly, as if struck by lightning. My jolting convulsion overcame me in a dazzling blaze of light. I yelped out like a squealing puppy and shivered all over, uncontrollably, like a leaf. I yelled again as another sudden burst hit me and in its jarring wake a second wave of joy swept over me like a hurricane."

She paused and swallowed hard before taking a sip of her drink. I felt my own excitement tightening my chest. I looked at her slender neck as the liquid went down her throat and my eyes dropped down again to the pink material of her panties, now even more visible between her slightly uncrossed legs. For a moment I wanted her to slip her fingertips beneath the material and show me how she had done it. I wanted to watch as her fingertips discovered the tip of her aching clitoris and I wanted to see her finish, so suddenly, so emphatically and I wanted my head filled with her screeching delight. I leant back and stretched to ease my tension. It was obvious what I was thinking.

"Was that the first time you had felt yourself?" I asked, pretending to be calm and objective.

"No, but it was the first time I had done it while thinking that someone must be watching. That was it you see. I was showing him what I was doing. I was slipping my fingers into my moist flesh so he could see. I was yelling out so he could hear. I was doing it all for him. My pleasure was for him."

"But you said no one came. You never saw the person who had written the note?"

"No, but it did not matter. I knew he was there you see, watching, listening."

She paused for a moment and bit on her lips. They whitened slightly against the pressure.

"The same day I left the school for good," she continued. "It had been arranged for me to go to a 'finishing' school in Switzerland. I had to fly to Geneva then travel by train to Chur where I was to be met. It was a long plane journey so I settled back, closed my eyes and listened to my Walkman. A steward brought my meal and when I lifted the plastic drinking cup from the tray there was a note beneath it. I looked around in amazement but saw no one suspicious or anyone taking any particular interest in me. The note told me to take the eye mask from my goodie bag, go into the loo behind me, but not lock the door. Inside, I was to stand facing the mirror, unbutton my shirt, drop my panties, pulling them no further down than my knees, put on the mask and wait. I could not believe it! For a few minutes I sat shivering, wondering what to do. The plane was full. It seemed ridiculous. How could I, how could anybody do that?"

I leant forward and took a drink from my glass. "Go on, go on," I urged, enthralled by her openness and now captivated by her exciting tale.

"There was something irresistible about it," she went on. "It had to be from the same person as before; I knew it. I was already certain he had watched me on the bench in the summerhouse, that he had heard me when I had screamed out in ecstasy and now, this same man was following me, watching my every move, thinking of things he could order me to do, planning out my life, prescribing my actions. I realised I no longer controlled my own destiny. All I could do was follow his instructions, take his orders and carry them out. I knew I could not resist. He had taken control of me.

"It was pretty scary, what he was telling me to do, and I was really frightened — all those people, the risk of being seen by them, of being discovered, found out, embarrassed — but the image which the note had put into my mind was all I could think about. I just had to do what I was told."

"So, you went to the loo and did what he said, undid your blouse, pulled your panties down, faced the mirror then put on the mask?"

"Yes. As soon as I could. I had to queue for ages to get in and several men pushed against me as I waited. I wondered if any of them was him but there was nothing to give me a clue. By the time I got in I was dying for a pee. I didn't know whether or not to lock the door while I went. I decided not to and I could hardly go for fear of someone opening the door. After I finished, I did what he said, got ready as he had instructed. I stood there for what seemed an age, all the time I was thinking of someone coming in and hauling me out, taking me to the captain or something ridiculous."

"You must have been terrified."

"I was shaking all over but I waited in exactly the way he had ordered. I had opened my blouse enough to see the tops of my breasts and I had my panties down precisely to where he had said. I leant forward slightly against the back of the loo, allowing my bottom to stick out a bit, hoping that it would be right. It seemed mad, worrying about exact details, but already I felt obsessed with doing precisely what he said. Then I heard the handle of the door being turned. It was as much as I could do to stay where I was. I bit my lips and waited for someone to start shouting, to drag me out, but all I heard was the door closing again as I felt the touch of a smooth hand on my exposed bottom."

"What happened? What did he do?"

"I was gasping as he touched me. It was as though the whole world was filled with nothing but his caress. My bottom seemed on fire as he slowly stroked it, first rubbing each cheek in a circular motion then letting his fingers drift up and down the cleft between them. I leant forward a little more and opened myself to him but he did not take advantage. So much I wanted him to delve his finger into my anus, or to open the labia of my sex, to thrust his fingers in, to squeeze my clitoris, whatever he wanted, but I could tell that what he wanted was none of those things. I realised my mouth was open and a dribble of spit was running over my bottom lip as his hand pulled away. I felt suddenly more exposed, exposed now to his gaze. I knew he was watching me, watching my excitement, witnessing my frustration. I wished he would spin me around and tear off my mask, rip my panties down over my ankles then grasp me around the thighs and lift me up, hold me above his stiffened cock and drop me onto it. Yes, I wanted to be seared by its heat, punished by its thrusting venous mass, and I wanted to drop heavily onto it in ecstasy as I felt the flow of his hot semen spurting deeply inside me, but all I heard was silence, all I felt was his stare. Then the door opened again but this time I did not hear it close, all I heard was the noise from the cabin beyond and I knew that he was exposing me to everyone out there. I bit my lips hard, it was so difficult to stay there, to do as he had instructed when I knew that he was showing me to everyone, degrading me, exposing me to public humiliation. I did not know how long I stayed there, I did not know how long he expected me to wait but, when I felt the hand of a stewardess on my shoulder I knew that I had done enough, done what he expected."

I looked at Zandra's blue eyes. They had lost their dreamy look. Now they were filled with brightness and clarity. The recollection of the incident had filled her again with excitement. It was sparking off her like electricity.

"What did you feel?" I asked expecting her to say how ashamed she had been, how embarrassed, how degraded.

"As I was taken back to my seat, with all those eyes on me, knowing that everyone had seen me like that, masked and semi-naked in the loo, I could not stop the rush of my orgasm. It would not end, it was like a flowing river. When I sat down and squeezed my buttocks together my flesh felt as if it had taken me over. I was completely consumed by it. It just would not stop. Tears ran down my cheeks and I shook for ages until, finally, it ebbed and I could close my eyes and relax."

"Did you see the man who had sent the note?"

"No," she said as though that confirmation itself filled her with a fresh burst of joy. "Everyone on the plane kept turning to look at me for the rest of the journey but their glares only thrilled me the more. The staff made me wait in the plane until everyone else had got off, I'm not sure why. Perhaps they thought I was a security risk! Everyone that got off took the chance to stare at me up close: women threw up their eyes, men grinned, someone even pulled at my hair. I slept on the train from Geneva and dreamed of what had happened. I woke up with my fingers deep inside my cunt. At Chur I was met by one of the older girls at the 'finishing" school, Greta. She was waiting at the end of the platform sitting on an old bicycle, her one leg stretched down to the pavement, the other bent up as she braced her foot on the pedal. She supported another bicycle with an extended hand that reached over lazily to the upswept handlebars. She was tall and blonde with full lips, beautiful white teeth and large blue eyes. She had square shoulders, slender arms and shapely legs and she wore a tightly buttoned pink vest tucked into a short, black, pleated sports skirt. On her feet were white trainers from one of which the laces dangled free. She threw her long hair back onto her bare, slightly freckled shoulders and waved her hand high as I got down from the train.

"Zandra!" she shouted. "Zandra!" as if she knew me.

Greta and I cycled side by side, like old friends, along the narrow streets of the ancient town of Chur, then out onto the tracks that wound through the sweet-smelling alpine meadows. Multicolored, iridescent clouds of butterflies rose up around us and we both laughed and shouted with glee as we sped, our feet off the pedals, down the grass-scented slopes which dropped in slow green folds towards the school. We rattled into the courtyard of the large complex — a mixture of ancient limestone buildings and wooden, A-frame chalets — both with our skirts blowing up in the wind, our panties creased around the bulbous fronts of the raised, leather saddles, our faces the very picture of excitement and delight.

The school was run by Herr and Frau Schwarz. Frau Schwarz taught us deportment and public speaking as well as arranging the frequent concerts and plays that the school put on for the local village. Herr Schwarz taught us horse riding and took us swimming in the nearby lake. Discipline was even stricter than it had been in the convent, we were not allowed to talk at meals and the slightest transgression led to some form of spanking or caning, sometimes in private and sometimes in front of the other girls. Still I kept receiving messages from my lord — that is what I decided to call him, my "unseen lord", it's my catholic upbringing I think. Sometimes letters came in the daily post, sometimes notes were left by my bed or handed to me by one of the maids or caretakers, but never once did I see him nor did I ever have any idea of who he might be. Once, when I was standing red-faced in front of Herr Schwarz as he disciplined me for not shining my riding boots properly, I even wondered if it was him. As I stood in the corner of his study facing the wall as he had instructed, and felt the warmth of his skin as he ran his fingers up between the backs of my thighs my heart began to race with expectant joy. When he widened my legs slightly, then peeled down my panties, leaving them crumpled up just above my knees, I felt sure it was my lord and I started to gasp as my stomach filled with excitement. But, as he started to rub his hands across my buttocks, I knew it was not him. His hands were too rough, too eager, then, as he probed between the cheeks of my bottom, sought out my anus and inserted his finger deeply into it before running the fingers of his other hand between my wet slit, I knew for certain that he was not my lord. My lord would not do such a thing. No, my lord would hold back, make me wait or order me to leave the room and expose myself to the other girls, so, even as Herr Schwarz took out his cock and spurted his hot semen over my bottom, I could only think of my lord, of how handsome he was and how he would treat me so differently. You see, since being in Switzerland, I had become familiar with my lord's cock. He would sometimes offer it to my mouth and let me slurp up his semen — he would let me take as much time as I had wanted until I was satisfied that I had got it all — but Herr Schwarz just let his semen run down between my legs, not allowing me to suck up any of it, not even letting me lick him at all.

Another time, one early, misty morning, as we all huddled in the boat house where we took off our clothes for swimming naked in the lake, Herr Schwarz scolded Greta for running too slowly to the water. She tried to avoid him, dodging to the side, but she slipped and he grabbed her and pulled her over his knee where he held her and whipped her with his riding crop. This was not my lord. My lord would never have been so cruel."

"What sorts of thing did he make you do, your lord?" I asked Zandra as the waiter brought another drink.

"Still does make me do," she corrected. "So many things, all delightful, all delectable, all so new, so forbidden, so liberating. He watches me of course, even when I don't hear from him for a while, I know he is still watching. Yes, he sees everything. Nothing I do is private from him, nothing. Sometimes he instructs me to go to places so that he can see me doing things in particular. When I was still in Switzerland, he sent me to Chur, to sit in a cafe and feel myself until I finished. Once he instructed me to wear a short fold-around skirt but no panties and to allow the skirt to come slightly open whenever I saw a man looking at me. Another time I had to take a job as a part-time waitress and encourage men to slip their hands up the skirt of my uniform or to bend over in such ways that they could see my panties. Sometimes he wants to touch me himself, but when he does he always makes me wear a mask, or a blindfold of some sort. He lets me suck his cock quite often and sometimes he sends me to meet young men so that they can have me in ways that he has already instructed them about. Sometimes they will pin me down and take me one by one, or perhaps they will tie me up and finish over me or in my mouth. Sometimes, I think he instructs them to do just what they want and he watches with special expectancy as they hold my legs apart, or whip me or make me suck them. Once he made some of them drag me into a public place and strip my clothes from me then leave me there, in the rain, alone. I think he enjoys seeing me most of all in that sort of way, naked, exposed, on display, in jeopardy."

"How do you come to be here?" I asked.

"He sends me instructions to travel to different places and when I get there he gives me further instructions. There is often money waiting for me or he encloses some with his directions. For the last six months he has sent me all over America. I have stood naked on the edge of the Grand Canyon with his semen dripping between my buttocks. I have knelt for hours, blindfolded and naked in the hot expanses of the Arizona Desert, until finally he allowed me to lap at his gushing cock. I have been trussed up by the wrists and ankles and suspended naked from the limb of a tree in the teeth of a Montana snow storm. Yet, even as I shivered in the biting cold I thrilled at the excitement of knowing he was watching and knowing I would have to endure it for as long as he wanted. I worked in a Nevada brothel, catering to the perverse needs of truck drivers and motor cyclists, until, only a few days ago, he sent a message ordering me to come here, to New Orleans. It came with an air ticket and instructions telling me to wear pink cotton panties and a short skirt. It said I would be met by a taxi and that I was to lie down in the back of it and pull my panties down so that the taxi driver could watch me masturbate in his mirror. Then, it said, I was to come here on New Year's Eve and wait for my next instruction so," she said smiling broadly, "here I am!" She slurped thirstily at her drink. "I am so excited," she continued. "So excited at the thought of what he has planned for me. I can never tire of his orders, never tire of submitting to his will. I am a virgin to everything he wishes. Everything he makes me do, I do as if for the first time. Everything I experience is for him and him alone. I cannot imagine any pleasure greater than the pleasure my unseen lord provides. Do you think it is wrong, to be controlled like this?" she asked almost plaintively.

"I'm not sure I know what it feels like," I said.

"Like nothing else on earth can feel like. It is like being born again, like watching the sunrise beyond the mountains, like swimming naked in the shimmering sheen of the moon in a warm alpine lake, it is like sipping the distilled nectar of an orgasm — it is like being in heaven. But," she said widening her eyes and cocking her head slightly to one side. "Even so, sometimes I wish I had someone to share it with. Yes, sometimes I wish I had a "sister" to share my ecstatic servitude." She swallowed hard. "Those men you saw me with. I thought it was them. I thought they were my lord's plan for me. I thought perhaps they were going to have me here in the bar, in public, but they left suddenly. Then," she hesitated, "then, I thought it might be you?" I laughed and shrugged then reached out and touched her hand. "Sometimes," she said squeezing my hand. "I really do wish I had a sister, a friend to share my pleasures with."

As I felt her fingers entwining with mine a thrill of excitement filled my stomach. I realised how excited I was by her situation, the constant unknowing, the continual expectation of the unfamiliar, the mystery of the uncontrolled and unpredictable future. She had no agreement, no contract, she had not even seen her lord, yet her obedience to him was so complete, so absolute. The more I thought of it, the more the idea of such servitude filled me with tremors of exhilaration and I squeezed her hand tightly, as if touching her would somehow bring me into contact with her obvious ecstasy.

The streets and alleys of the French Quarter, the Vieux Carré — spinning out in a web of body-filled filaments from the central, bustling Bourbon Street —

buzzed with noise and clamour as party-goers, fresh with excitement from the fireworks and Mardi Gras, the dancing, the whistles, the hubbub and Creole excitement, poured back into the waiting bar. The waiter brought another tray of drinks. He nodded to both of us and offered Zandra a closely folded note.

"For you mademoiselle," he said bowing and handing her the note.

Zandra looked around eagerly, as if even though her lord had always been invisible to her, this time she might just catch a glimpse of him. I looked around as well, sharing her naive expectancy. But there was nothing unusual to be seen, everyone was involved in their own lives, drinking, talking, laughing, embracing.

"What does it say?" I asked, eagerly sitting forward to see the note. She unfolded it slowly. It was written in a careful hand with neatly formed letters. "What does it say?"

"It says, 'Leave your new friend. Go into the next cubicle. Kneel down on one of the benches and pull your panties down'."

A thrill like no other I had ever felt ran through me. It was actually happening, here, now! I could hardly believe it. Her story was true and was still unfolding. And he had seen me! He was watching me as well! All of a sudden I was struck by the thrilling sense of fear that came with the instructions. How could anyone be so obedient? How could anyone expose themselves like that, in public, here, now?" My stomach churned and, as I breathed heavily with expectant gasps of fear, I felt a heat inside me and a wetness running against the hot swelling flesh of my aching labia.

I watched Zandra carefully fold the note and put it

inside her small bag. She squeezed my hand again then got up and went into the next cubicle. I could not take my eyes off her. I could see that she was thinking of nothing except doing what her lord said. There was no one in the cubicle, everyone was standing up shouting, chatting, drinking. She climbed onto one of the wooden benches and knelt down just as she had been told. I felt my face flushing, I could not believe she was doing it. She hitched up her skirt until it was around her waist then, slowly and without any fear, she pulled down her panties. People started looking at her, pointing, then the four men I had seen her with originally came into the cubicle. The tall one stood in front of her and undid his trousers and, while she took his heavy cock unhesitatingly into her mouth, one of the others began licking the already glistening flesh between her legs. The other two stood on each side of her, one feeling her breasts and pinching her nipples, the other wrapping his arm around her waist and lifting her bottom as high as possible. The man licking her cunt stood back, took his heavy, swollen cock in his hand then drove it into her now sopping flesh.

Everyone in the bar was captivated as the scene unfolded. Each man took a turn, moving around her, sharing out her delights and, as each finished inside her she threw her head back and screamed out, a wild, uncontrolled screech of uninhibited delight. I ran my fingers around my breasts and felt my hard, throbbing nipples then, as I squeezed them tightly in an effort to stem my growing ecstasy, I felt a body behind me. At first he simply pressed closer than he should, then he pressed intentionally against my buttocks, then he wrapped his hands around the front of my hips. I did nothing to stop him as his warm hands pressed into the indentations on the inside edges of my hip bones then, maintaining the pressure, he let them run down the fronts of my trembling thighs. He, this stranger, turned his palms outwards and brought them up, with their backs together, between my legs until they touched, so lightly, the crotch of my panties. I did not look away from Zandra. I did not think to see who was touching me.

"Pull them down," he said in my ear. "Not all the way, just above your knees."

My stomach filled with excitement. He pulled his hands away and I did what he said. It was as though there was no alternative, no choice, I simply had to obey his instructions. He stood back and, when I let go of my panties, he lifted my skirt until the hem was resting at my waist. My bottom was full exposed and I did not know who was watching or what would happen next. I let my fingers slip between my legs but as soon as I felt their tips probing between my pubic hair, seeking out the crack of my flesh, tantalising my clitoris, I was overcome with the onrush of a sudden, devastating orgasm. I threw my head back and, as if released like a wild animal set free from a cage, I screamed at the top of my voice as the paroxysms ran through me in a massive, jerking, convulsive flood.

As I pushed myself out of the cubicle I bumped into the waiter. Still shaking with excitement, I squeezed past him, raising my arms high in the air as he lifted his tray above his shoulder. As we sashayed past each other, my nostrils filled with a sweet fragrance. It was the scent of my own juices — the sweet, delicate fragrance of my own sexuality on his hands — and, as I looked for Zandra amongst the renewed crowds that flooded in from the hectic streets of the noisy, celebrating town, I knew that her 'unseen lord' had a new slave and Zandra, a new sister.

Syra Bond's other novels are; 'The Roman Slave Girl' and 'The Trojan Slaves'..

The Nun's Chronicle

By Falconer Bridges

This is an extract from the forthcoming novel 'The Caning Chronicles'.

Sister Cecelia's cunt was on fire.

And it was all my doing.

I'd slashed, beaten and ravaged almost every inch of her lithe, enticingly unspoilt body until her entire being pulsed and burned with the raging passion that only a proficient and thorough chastisement can achieve. As each successive, biting stroke had fallen, much like an alchemist turning base metal into gold, I'd slowly and steadily engineered the mutation of one state of existence into another. But what I had transformed was something altogether different. I had converted almost unendurable pain into almost unendurable pleasure: a feat of pure sorcery of which only the most accomplished and experienced Masters of punishment are capable.

Of course I'd paid a great deal of attention to her breasts before I'd moved on to her garden of veiled delights. Veiled, I hasten to add, not by the coarse cloth habit that was her normal apparel, but by something altogether more sensuous and pleasurable to the eye. Her vaginal lips and the entrance to her love hole were almost hidden by the extraordinarily dense, long and silky cunt hairs that sprouted from her well-thatched and prominent 'Mound of Venus'. And a most satisfying and eminently prick rousing sight it was, especially to any man who prefers to gaze upon a naked female in her natural state, rather than is the fashion among many noble ladies of shaving every hair from their bodies. And like those men, shaven cunts are not to my taste.

I cannot deny that throughout the session of breast punishment I had been aching to get on with what I enjoy more than anything else - the thrashing of a previously innocent and untutored sex. But most enjoyable and satisfying as that is, first things must come first. And so I had gained as much delight as I could by demonstrating what surely would have been considered by anyone able to watch it, a master tutorial in the art of the flailing of breasts. When delivered by myself that is a tit torture quite the equal of the insertion of embroidery needles, the clamping of the full mammary in a screwed-down press or the piercing of the nipples with leather-working bodkins.

Of course to be considered on a par with the more usually accepted torment that those tortures of the breasts produce, I reasoned that I must submit my techniques and methods to the appraisal of my peers.

And that I have done.

So I am proud to disclose that not a single of my so-called equals has ever considered themselves able to challenge my superior ability. My true equal they will never be - I am the Grand Master, the ultimate exponent of flagellation, the prophet whose teachings must be followed to the letter.

And as I do not suffer from false modesty, I have no hesitation in declaring myself to be the ultimate expert in the deliverance of pleasurable pain. Countless years of practice had honed my skills to such perfection that failure to thrash an inexperienced novice to orgasm was something that neither I nor any member of The Brethren was able to contemplate. For that reason, although I was brought to that forbidding and sombre place solely for the training of Sister Cecelia, having realised my special qualifications, the Prioress always called upon me to introduce the new initiates of her Order to the delights that physical discipline and corporal punishment can bring into their lives.

The heights to which I was able to take them were legendary in the Convent. So much so that following their initiation by myself, many of the sisters never again found themselves able to attain the same pinnacle of fulfilment to which I drove them at their induction ceremony. Time and again they begged the Prioress to allow them to taste my cutting bite once again, only to be told that their initial time with me was a holy-ordained foretaste of the delights that await them in Heaven if they remain true to their vows.

To experience such gratification again the sisters were required to pledge their hearts, souls and physical bodies to the 'One True God'. I hardly need to add that this solemn promise of course included the nuns' spiritual brothers, the monks of the priory. Mortal men who are His flesh and blood representatives here on Earth. And this they always did. Every last one of them, in the hope that I would once again lead them along the road to sexual paradise. The spiritual paradise promised by The Almighty himself faded into mere inconsequence when they recalled the heavenly journey on which I conducted them. Once I had converted them to believe in my own doctrine, that the gaining of divine recognition, as well as the pleasure of immeasurably mind-bending and body-racking orgasms is attainable only through pain, they lived for nothing else.

How easy it was for me. How absolutely impossible it was for them. Those unworldly women, noviciates and nuns alike, found themselves completely unable to deny my power and authority. They had little concept of anything that existed beyond the realms of their overheated imaginations. Virtually imprisoned in the convent, they were confined there, ignorant and shackled by religion. Oft times it was because they had imagined themselves called thither by His voice, but more often than not it was upon the wishes of parents eager to rid themselves of unwanted daughters. Daughters who did nothing but bleed their households of what little resources they had. So by one means or another those unfortunate souls sought succour behind the walls of the convent. Marriage to God was their salvation, their cocoon from the harsh realities of the outside world that were so luridly described to them by the Abbot and the Prioress.

The outside world? What was that? They knew not. But me, before I was brought to that place I had slashed, beaten and scourged my way through all the forbidden pleasures of the flesh so expressly forbidden by the scriptures. Scriptures totally ignored by both the nuns of the convent in which I found myself and the monks of their associated monastery.

As I recall those halcyon days of yore, I cannot give any real account of the number of times I had found myself almost drowning in the juices of love, buried up to the hilt in a spasming, gripping cunt. Suffice to say it is many times in excess of anything even the most active of cocks can normally expect to experience. So many were the grateful, lusting maids that I drove to a flooding, convulsing climax that I gained a notoriety that eventually saw me welcomed into the households of a multitude of the great and good.

As tales of my indisputable prowess filtered continually down and then back up through the structured social layers of noblemen, gentry, freemen and serfs, sexually denied or mistreated men of every rank utilised my services to bring haughty wives, concubines and daughters to heel. And in doing so I came to learn that the fables regarding their cosseted ladies that great knights and patricians seek to impress upon their underlings are completely without foundation. The bodies of aristocratic females are no more sweet, tender or desirable than those of a well-scrubbed peasant girl, a tavern wench or guttersnipe whore. In truth, upon reminiscing I find that a buxom well-fucked tart, who makes her daily bread through the selling of her cunt, arse, mouth and tits, will almost always provide infinitely greater satisfaction to a lust-driven hard and throbbing cock than any of those interbred sexless products of formally-arranged marriages.

Since the earliest of my days here in the land of Albion, introducing both masters and slaves to the intricacies of sexual dominance has been my calling. Throughout the seemingly endless spunk-filled years, I have been called upon by my masters to thrash and then invade not only the cunts of maidens of their own paramountcy but also those of innocent girls of low-born status. Maidens plucked from villages or fields without fear of retribution, their lord's 'Droit de Seigneur' being not open to challenge.

Many of the younger nobles were completely inexperienced and knew nothing of sex; of the gushingly drinkable, tongue-delighting musky juices that flood from a raging, orgasming vagina. But my experience is without parallel and after a period of association with me, every single one of them would tell you without fear of contradiction that maids from the gutter fuck, suck, smell better and generally provide more pleasure than a titled lady could ever contemplate. Which is why for a bollock-bursting and thoroughly satisfying fuck, they are forever the choice of high-born men.

As dutiful subjects of the Crown and loyal servants of your own lord, what a sad duty it is of mine to enlighten you to facts that may cause you to doubt the veracity of your betters. They do not wed for love, or even lust. Noblemen marry Noblewomen because it is their expected duty. And that duty is to sire a legitimate heir, born of the aristocracy, to carry forward their names and titles. An heir who will inherit their estates and chattels, its sire usually engaging in only the most perfunctory sexual congress in order to accomplish this feat. In truth as the result of centuries of interbreeding, aristocratic females are more often than not extremely plain in appearance, something that does little to tempt a lusty cock into fucking them for pleasure and satisfaction.

And more pleasure and satisfaction have I been witness to than it would be wise to admit. The rock hard shafts of revered Knights, dribbling with the liquor that comes before the actual penetration of an eager dripping cunt, is a sight that is not uncommon to me. And in truth these 'Defenders of The Faith' are rarely content to make use of only one maiden at a time. More often than not, following a sound thrashing from myself to prepare the girls properly for the favour of being allowed to sexually service their masters, these warriors will fuck and sodomise two, three or even more lusty cocksuckers. And when the fucking is over, with myself close at hand, it is often a knight's delight to sit with a goblet of wine held to his lips, observing the receptacle of his newly planted seed standing with her skirts held high and her legs spread wide, allowing the combined juices of the cock and the cunt to trickle from the lips of her still wide-open and well-filled hole. Sticky globules of cloudy-white sap dripping from a wench's scabbard and falling either to the ground or into the eager open mouth of one of her naked prostrate acolyte companions is an experience so common that I really am no longer able to pay it any great attention.

Spunk.

Cunts.

Cocks.

I love those words. And I love to see them written down, which is a rare occurrence as the few men who have the knowledge of writing are usually holy men, monks and the like. But nevertheless, as unbelievable as it would seem, there in the Prioress' private rooms I saw the most unusual of books. A real manuscript written in Latin by an educated hand not afraid of the words of condemnation uttered by the lackies of Rome. This book told of the sight of a withdrawn cock, at the moment of ejaculation, spurting a fountain of foaming white sperm high into the air. Of this sperm saturating both the fucker and the fucked with a shower of the glorious elixir of life. It tells of how that elixir, the liquor a free man manufactures, is stored in his bollocks until it is wrenched out as he reaches the climax of his lovemaking. That is where I learned that unless she is desperate to find herself in child, a man's spurting spunk is ambrosia women would rather have poured into their mouths than their cunts. To taste, to savour and to swallow, that is their desire.

And while they are often not backward in confessing to their masters that a spurting, throbbing cock stuffed deep into their mouths is a dream being fulfilled, there is another more common desire that women find great difficulty in expressing.

And that desire is for pain.

Exquisite nerve-tingling, cunt-paralysing pain. The forbidden pleasure. The nipple-hardening, brain-softening ecstasy that results from the unbridled correction administered by their masters; aided more often than not by others of my kind. We are the keys that open the portals into paradise, the joy bringers who meld desire, suffering and bliss into one glorious whole and offer enlightenment to all womankind. To ask is to receive. No true man would stay his hand and deny a begging maid a thorough thrashing, if that is what she needs to propel her into a state of rapture.

And that is exactly the service that I was performing for Sister Cecelia, although it would be a falsehood to claim that it was she who had actually called for the chastisement. No, that had been the Prioress. It seems that the Abbot was constantly complaining that although she had been installed in the convent for many a month, Sister Cecelia had not as yet made her cunt or arse available to him or his congregation of monks. In fact he had not even so much as cupped her breasts or felt his hot throbbing rod slipping between her cool wet lips into her mouth. Accompanying him into her presence one day, I was privy to their conversation. The Abbot was displeased, that much even I could discern.

"Young blood, that is what I need. A fresh unspoilt maid such as Cecelia skewered on the end of my prong. My mouth suckling her newly-ripe nipples as I slide in and out of her tender body. The smell of her cunt. The taste of it too. Her tongue roving over my shaft. Her pale white fingers ringing my bell-end, wanking me to a spurting climax. God's teeth woman, these things I need, nay I demand. As Father of this community they are my right and it is your duty to provide them."

The Abbot's words were filled with anger, his lust overwhelming his vow of celibacy, as it had done countless times before. But the Prioress' reply was not all that forthright. I could tell that she was desperately seeking some way out. Some way of not allowing Cecelia's flesh to be the feast to satisfy his carnal hunger.

"The girl has not been with us all that long and you have all the others of my flock available for your use."

The Prioress' words were earnest if not altogether believable.

"And I have used them all time and time again until now most of them no longer rouse the serpent beneath my cassock. Even splayed over the altar, with their legs wide and holes open, many are the times that my rod has not filled with iron enough for me to enter them. But Cecelia, I could fuck her in an instant."

The Abbot's reply however was truthfully forthright. But still the Prioress seemed hesitant to grant his demands.

"My Lord Abbot, she is the youngest of our noviciates and not yet ready to be introduced to the beast that hangs between your thighs. I am sure that with more preparation from myself she will in time reach that point. But she is not there yet and knows nothing of sex. That knowledge I must impart to her. I have to teach her through love and gentle persuasion that her sex hole and her arse hole are the keys to eternal bliss and salvation."

It was then that the light began to dawn on me. It was not as if I had not seen the signs. The Prioress wanted to keep Cecelia solely for herself! And if I had made that deduction, then the Abbot most certainly had too. But he did not know as I did, that Sister Cecelia was not as untouched and pure as the Prioress was implying. With some assistance from me she had been sampling the young nun's sexual delights for quite some time.

Sometimes it had been in Cecelia's stark, sparsely furnished cell. At other times in the Prioress' more opulent quarters and more than once out in the open fields or in the orchard. With her coarse robe pulled up above her waist, I had slashed into Sister Cecelia's naked buttocks or stung her tits and cunt until she was gushing love juice and well prepared for the Prioress' attentions.

And the Prioress was nothing if not inventive in her use of the girl. The smaller of the ornate candlesticks were often pushed deep into her most private holes; substitutes for the smooth polished wooden dildos the nuns more usually used on each other. One of her favourite sex games was to lay Cecelia down and insert the candle holder into her tight, dripping cunt and then, squatting astride her, ram the base of the candlestick into her own much slacker hole. Frantically rubbing her erect love kernel, she would bounce up and down, writhing and moaning as she drove herself to a most unholy climax, shrieking out her thanks to the lord when a shuddering orgasm finally raged over her.

Once or twice Cecelia herself was reduced to what was in effect a squirming, palpitating piece of sexual wreckage, as to her what were unfathomable brain-melting sensations, raged within her innocent body and left her convulsing in ecstasy. The Prioress did not seem to be overly concerned on those occasions. The novice's fulfilment was none of her concern after all. So although she made no effort to ensure that Cecelia gained any satisfaction from their carnal conjunctions, if the girl did actually find some sort of fulfilment, then the Prioress thought that that would help to bind Cecelia to her.

Cecelia's tongue was also something the Prioress had made great use of, whether ordering her to suck the great projectile nuggets that sprouted from her huge udders or making her lap the sagging, swimming sex lips that dangled from her vulva. The Prioress' instructions were never anything less than straight to the point.

"Get that tongue in further girl, right up to the root!

Make me feel it wriggling deep inside me. Pleasure me well if you wish for my indulgence and protection."

And Sister Cecelia always obeyed such orders without question. After all this woman was the holy Mother Superior and would never require her to do anything that was unholy in the eyes of God.

If the Abbot had been privy to that secret knowledge then I am certain that his rage would have known no bounds. As it was there was menace in his voice as he continued his angry harassment of the Prioress.

"The girl is over the age of consent, you cannot deny that."

Furious at the Prioress' attempts to deter him from his quest to fuck and thrash Cecelia, the Abbot's angry, accusing words cut her to the core. I could sense the conflict raging within her. She had been savouring the taste of Sister Cecelia's cunt, and had herself been on the receiving end of her searching tongue and enjoying all manner of sexual delights almost from the moment that she entered the convent. But that was something that, try as she may, the Prioress would not be able to keep secret forever. So eventually, stung by the Abbot's persistent disgruntled carping, she decided that the time had come for me to introduce Cecelia to the ultimate fulfilment that her continuing virginity denied her.

After all, that was my only reason for being in the convent. Cecelia was the youngest daughter of a great lord, and as such had been very guardedly kept a virgin until she became of an age when she could be consigned to the care of the Sisters of Mercy; that being her father's bound duty to the crown and the holy Church of Rome. The lord knew full well that his offspring was being delivered into a life of sexual slavery, but that was the way of the world. And being a prolific and enthusiastic wielder of his child maker, he had daughters to spare. One given over to the debased usage of the monks was neither here nor there. And if it ensured the continued absolution of his many sins, then the loss of a hardly-noticed female product of his loins was a small price to pay.

And that absolution had been guaranteed to him by the Abbot, provided that Cecelia provided good service to the cocks of himself and his hooded underlings. Although of course he made no admission of the fact, the lord was not entirely certain that she would provide the required satisfaction. And although I was not particularly happy with the situation, that was the reason that when he had her delivered to the convent I was sent along with her. I had given him many years of exemplary service and he trusted me beyond question. I was to be the enforcer. The rod that bent her to her new master's will. If she proved not to be fully pliant and did not live up to the Abbot's expectations, then I was to do what I do best – thrash her into willing submission.

And so the scene was set. The witnesses were assembled in the chapel according to tradition, the monks on one side of the aisle and the sisters on the other. There was no moon in the pitch blackness of the overcast sky of night and except for intermittent flashes of forked lightning, not the faintest ray of light filtered through the stained glass of the windows to offer even the slightest natural illumination. The wild wind battered the thick stone walls of the chapel and thunder the like of which I had never experienced before, shook the building to its foundations. The atmosphere was eerily tense and expectant and the air lay heavy and thick with the sooty smoke of the ceremonial candles; their flickering yellow glow fighting a losing battle with the gloom that crept into every corner.

Standing by the altar, with me once again by his side, the Abbot impatiently awaited Sister Cecelia's arrival.

"God's teeth," I heard him mutter. "Am I to be kept waiting 'til doomsday. Where is that confounded woman?"

The Prioress, for it was she to whom he was referring, entered the chapel at that very moment. A heavy silver cross was held high in her left hand and a leash of plaited bull hide clasped tightly in her right. Attached to the other end of the leash was a wide leather collar, studded with iron spikes and that collar was clamped tightly around the pure white skin of Sister Cecelia's neck.

A Sister Cecelia whom I had never dreamt could have existed.

Towed by the leash, her hair brushed and falling loose, her lips coloured red and with her wrists manacled behind her back, she followed several paces behind the Prioress as she made her way towards the altar and the Abbot.

And what a sight she was. Prepared with the greatest of care and attention especially for this momentous occasion by the Prioress herself, the shapeless nun's habit had been ripped from her back, revealing the gleaming, oiled and sweet-scented body of an angel. Stripped naked, her breasts stood full and proud, with broad hazelnut areola encircling enormous nipples of mouth-watering perfection. Perhaps it was the biting cold teasing them into erection, but be that as it may, those nipples were the most perfect in Christendom. Her waist was slender, her hips curved and she had an arse that could make a man weep for the want of sinking his weapon into it. Loins, long and slender, led a watcher's gaze to the succulent mound of her sex that lay between them. It can be justly said that there was not a single human being in the chapel whose eye fell upon her, male or female, whose pulse did not grow faster as carnal desire swept through his or her lusting body.

Halting before the altar and the Abbot, in a faltering voice the Prioress turned to Sister Cecelia.

"The sin must be thrashed from your body, your soul cleansed and your virginity sacrificed to God before you may be accepted fully into our order. That has been the way for centuries and all of us here, including myself have undergone this ritual to prepare ourselves for admittance to The Lord's Holy Paradise. The Abbot is The Lord's representative here in our community and so the duty of preparing you for Divine acceptance falls upon him."

I have been on this Earth for countless long years, sometimes maintaining an association with 'The Church' and sometimes not, but I knew full well that the Prioress' words were false. They were just a means to convince a naïve young girl to surrender her holes, her mouth and her all to the carnal desires of a lust-filled Abbot and his equally sexually avaricious cohort of iniquitous, sin-filled monks. Nevertheless, under the Abbot's direction, I thrashed and whacked, feeling her taut flesh ripple under the impact as every full-blooded stroke drove the breath from her lungs and the screams from her mouth. And the joy was more than I am able to relate. For me as well as for her. This was the reason for my very existence and I drank in her every moan, screech and cry of ecstasy until I felt intoxicated by my power. Full of exhilaration I revelled in the delight of just being what I am: the instrument of correction and obedience. Once more I could not go wrong. Despite the devilish cold I was bringing the understanding of Man's power and dominion over women to yet another welcoming mind.

And a true joybringer I proved to be yet again as her passions rose with every slice into her meaty haunches, every cut across the Venusian mounds of her breasts and every drive between her spread thighs. Droplets of her musky juices splattered onto her belly, drove themselves down the insides of her legs and even flew wildly into the cold air, some falling upon the Abbot's hard and straining cock. Reaching down, he wiped them from his manhood with circled fingers and raising them to his mouth, savoured the pungent, heady taste of her cunt. The jolt that imparted to his cock was impossible to miss and I knew the time was near when he would be unable to restrain himself any further and would leap upon her with the sexual fervour of a demented devil.

I knew him of old and 'man of the church' or otherwise, when it came to fucking, he was as insatiable and demonic as the Devil himself. And so I had to make the very utmost of my final moments of pleasure, doubling my energies and inventiveness to ensure that Sister Cecelia would never forget the magic moment when I delivered her enlightenment and she was presented to 'God's chosen cock'.

That moment arrived far sooner than I would have wished. The Abbot suddenly thrust me aside and with his cock clasped into his fist like a battering ram, lunged at Sister Cecelia and speared her with one giant thrust into her soaking cunt. As she lay backwards over the altar, her legs spread wide, his throbbing, pulsing weapon drove half its length into her at his first assault. Her shocked but exultant scream bounced from bare stone wall to bare stone wall, echoing the length and breadth of the crowded chapel.

At his second thrust, his ramrod completely disappeared into her clasping vagina and he fell on top of her, ramming and reaming with the abandoned wildness of a lust-crazed bull servicing a hapless cow. And what a cow Sister Cecelia proved herself to be. A human cow, begging and screaming to be fucked insensible.

"Fuck me harder master. Hurt me please! The Prioress is right, only a merciless ravaging by a Holy prick and the blessed pain of the sacred cane can purify my soul. Oh, please fuck me 'til you have fucked away each and every one of my sins."

Her udders heaved beneath his fat, sweating body as only too eager to grant her desperate plea, he clasped his hands under her buttocks and pulled her even further onto his over-used, wart-covered cock. Oblivious to his wrinkled ugliness and rampant with sexual hunger, she dug her fingernails into the flabby flesh of his back and clamped her legs around his waist in an effort to ensure that the solid rod of throbbing gristle stuck deep inside her could not be pulled from its joyous host until it had fucked her into the heaven she had been promised.

Oh how I wished that it was me anchored tight in her foaming cunt, her love juices pouring over me as I wallowed in that mystical tunnel of desire, soaking up every drop of her flooding come. But alas that was not to be. The Abbot was fucking it and he was going to keep on fucking it until he had fucked it senseless. So all I could do was watch. Watch every plunge of his shagstick in and out of her honeypot as I fell deeper and deeper into a well of misery as I saw her being stoked up into a brazier of fiery dementia.

How a repulsive ale-soaked barrel of lard such as the Abbot could reduce a maiden as fair as Cecelia to a writhing wreck of carnal hunger still remains a mystery to me. And hungry she was. Even after he finally reached a grunting, breathless climax and I saw his fat arse jerking uncontrollably between her wide-spread thighs as he shot spurt after spurt of hot spunk deep into her hole, she still wanted more.

"Oh Lord Abbot, do not stop now. Please! Keep on fucking me. Sodomise me. Stick your cock in my mouth. Do anything you want, but please do not stop."

The words were gasped out as she fought for breath, seemingly hardly able to speak as the tremors engulfed her body. And there was more.

"Shoot your spunk on my belly. Shoot it into my mouth and up my arse. Wipe it over my face and dry your holy shaft in my hair. Oh happy me, never in my most secret of dreams could I have hoped that service to the Church would bring such blissful delight."

It was then that a long recognised realism swept over me. Women are nothing but strumpets. Whores! Any stiff cock that is able to propel them into orgasm is welcome to burrow into their most private of holes. They care nothing for devotion. Genuine feelings harboured by their most fervent admirers are cast aside when they feel a boiling cock reaming them into orgasm. And the Abbot was doing just that. She thought of me not. And as one of her most ardent devotees, I reeled in misery as I was forced to accept that I meant nothing to her. If I had possessed a heart then it would have been broken asunder.

Such is my miserable existence.

Broken hearts are not for such as me. I have specific duties to perform and perform them I do to the absolute best of my abilities. Mayhap that is the reason that I prove to be so viciously extreme in my chastisement of innocent flesh. If I cannot enjoy the sexual pleasure that I induce, that being left to whatever master I am serving, then I may as well enjoy to the full the sight of writhing, tortured flesh as I lash into it.

And enjoy it I did.

The Abbot would have carried on fucking and buggering her no matter what, but the wild abandon of her pleas for more seemed to spur him on to even greater excess. And for that he once again was in need of my assistance.

Pulling his malodorous knob from her dripping sex purse, he pushed his podgy paws under her hip bones and heaved her over onto her belly, before dropping her face down over the altar. Gasping, he turned to the Prioress.

"She loves the cock. And she loves the cane. This wench is greatly to my liking and I am going to make sure that she gets her fill of both."

Then with his straining shaft swinging hither and thither in front of the paunch of his belly, he set me to work once more.

With her arse thrust high and the juices of love, the Abbot's as well as hers, running down the insides her thighs, Sister Cecelia was as near perfect for a thrashing as perfect can be. Under the Abbot's direction, firstly I lashed her buttocks. Hard! Weal after weal layered itself over the fiery striations I had inflicted earlier. Squeal after ecstatic squeal burst from her mouth, together with the foulest of words. Words that I would never have believed such a previously delicate and innocent virgin would have any knowledge of.

And the Abbot was not wrong. She did love the cane. It seemed as if she just could not get enough and so he directed me to her vagina. He widened her legs to give me easier access, his eyes glistening in appreciation as I whipped up between them to land a numbing strike to her vulva. Still hanging open, wet and sticky from the Abbot's frantic shagging, her sex lips sucked and squelched as if she were trying to permanently imprison the miraculous thrill of my strike within her lusting hole.

I pulled free and struck again, once more sinking between her dripping labia. Her squeals turned to howls as I continued to punish her. Strike after strike, howl after howl until she suddenly stiffened and pushing her arse backwards to meet my next strike, she shook and jerked as if possessed by a demon. Wailing and praising the Lord she lost all control as the most raging orgasm I have ever been privy to witness overwhelmed her.

Ululating, grunting, laughing and crying all at the

same time, she collapsed against the altar. Her trembling legs seemed to lose all their strength and she slid down to cold floor and lay in a twitching heap of arms and legs.

"Well done my friend. Without any doubt, you have surpassed yourself. You serve me well."

Much appreciated as they were, those words from the Abbot came as a great surprise. Ill-tempered as he was, words of praise from him were very few and far between. But I was not allowed to bask in my glory for long.

"Now once again it is the turn of the cock!"

Clamping both hands around his pulsing shaft, he turned around in a full circle, showing the monstrous beast to the entire congregation. Loosening one hand, he made a great show of pointing down and drawing the eyes of the assembly to its juice-and-spunk-covered length.

"This Cock!"

Those two words were almost shouted. Not only the sin of lust but also the sin of gluttony was sweeping over him; his dissolute senses feasting to the full on Sister Cecelia's physical pain and sexual downfall. Once again he addressed the Prioress.

"Get her back up on her feet. I cannot fuck her while she is lying on the floor like some swooning delicate lady of the Court."

Summoning the assistance of two of the sisters, the Prioress hauled Sister Cecelia up from the floor and planted her on unsteady feet before the Abbot.

"Now girl, I am going to give you the most wondrous of fuckings. The fucking that you have been begging for. Prepare yourself and savour it well. But first tell me again how much you desire me to screw my holy prong into your undeserving cunt."

And so she did, using almost the same words as when she had first begged him to fuck her arse and her cunt. The Abbot urged her on to ever more extreme demands until finally he signalled her to stop.

"Enough. I think we all know now how much you yourself delight in the sins of the flesh. So now I am going to grant your wishes. As my first gift, my cock will attend to your arse, and believe me that will be something you will never forget. Your shitter will welcome me as Mother Mary welcomed the Angel. And after I am done, you will believe forever that the hole in your backside was placed there by God purely to satisfy the carnal needs of men.

"Cunts are one thing: spunk shot deep into them more often than not results in the production of one more unwelcome howling infant. On the other hand, spunk shot deep into an arse allows for no such outcome. And for a man the pleasure is just the same, in fact even more so because arse fucking is strictly forbidden by the scriptures.

"And when I have spunked my all into you and can spunk no more, I am going to string you up from that rafter above you and call upon all of my flock to give you the beatings and fuckings of all lifetimes. No woman will ever have been fucked as much as you. One after another they will fuck you until the spunk runs in rivers from your holes and your mouth. Is that not cause for rejoicing?"

It was not.

That much I could tell by the shocked look on Sister Cecelia's face. No answer passed her lips.

"Come now girl! What is wrong? You pleaded for the cock, did you not? You begged to be fucked again and again and so be transported to paradise. We all heard you. So once more I ask you: what is wrong?"

Sister Cecelia's voice was weak and faltering as she finally confessed her fears.

"My Lord Abbot, there are so many of them. I am afraid they will hurt me."

"That is possible. But you like pain. You have told me as much. And the pleasure that their cocks bring you will numb your body to the hurt. Now, rejoice in what is to come. My blessings be upon you."

Seemingly in some response to his words, the Abbot's ramrod swelled to unbelievable dimensions as he pushed her forwards and ordering her to touch her toes, drove it deep into her backside. Rocking on her feet against his inhuman onslaught, she fought to keep from being toppled over as he thrust again and again into her arse. Grunting, sweating and cursing, he withdrew his throbbing lance from her clasping shithole, before ever and again plunging back in with a determination that beggared belief. The Abbot was a man on a mission. A mission to fuck Cecelia into a state of existence so wonderful that afterwards she would never think twice about obeying any sexual demand he or any of his disciples made upon her.

I cannot describe my feelings as I watched him and his cohort fuck, beat and thrash Sister Cecelia incessantly for what seemed, and probably was, hours. Her cunt, her mouth and her arse were filled time and time again with rock hard cocks, candles and all manner of penetrative devices.

And of course, oceans of spunk!

It ran down her thighs. It dripped from her nose. It emerged in frothy streams from between her lips, even when her mouth was full of cock; the spunk having been spurted into her by the previous violator. She shook, she shuddered and she screamed when she was able – sometimes in torment, but ever and again in the ecstasy of orgasm. And she never again begged for mercy – she loved every moment.

All she wanted was more.

More cock.

More teeth sinking into her breasts and biting her nipples.

More monks spurting their seed over her naked body.

More pain!

And all I wished for was to be able to join in. To be able to experience the same communion of ecstasy that they all were. But that was not possible. Why? Why must I always be alone? Excluded. It was me who had stoked her into a raging hunger for sexual fulfilment. Me who had driven her to beg to be fucked. Me who had paved the way for the Abbot to indulge in any and every perversion he desired.

It was all so unfair.

I was drowning in desolation as I finally realised that I would not be called upon again to aid in their unholy rampage. And rampage they did. All of them. As I had been, the nuns had been driven to desperation by the frenzied sight before their eyes. They wanted to be fucked as well. Robes fell in heaps all over the chapel as they wrenched off their coverings and ran to the rampant monks. Cocks stuffed themselves deep into drenching cunts. Mouths clamped around other spurting shafts and an unbelievable orgy of sexual excess erupted to fill the chapel with a screaming, wailing and thrashing throng of sinful and depraved holy children of God.

They were so taken up with each other that Sister Cecelia found herself abandoned and without a cock stuck into any of her holes. But not for long! The Abbot saw to that. Once again he pounced and drove his warty weapon deep into her overflowing love casket.

Then suddenly without warning, the heavy doors of the chapel burst asunder and a rearing steed of war, clad in full battle armour with a unicorn's horn of steel strapped around his forehead thundered through them. On his back he carried a mighty knight, his own armour covered by a black cloak with an eight-pointed Maltese cross sewn on to it; the battle gown of the Knights of St John of Jerusalem. Even though his face was hidden by his lowered visor, just one glance was sufficient for me to recognise who he was: Sister Cecelia's lord and father, Sir Mortimer D'Arcy DuPont!

So now he had adopted the guise of a Hospitaller. At the time he delivered Cecelia and myself to the convent, his uniform had been a white tunic with a red latin cross on the back; the insignia of The Poor knights of Christ – the Knights Templar – who were anything other than poor. But in reality I knew that he was neither of those things, he was altogether more special; the head of 'The Brotherhood of The Sons of Adam', a mysterious secret organisation that was the hidden power behind Kings and Emperors the world over and in reality had ruled the Earth since its creation.

With his broadsword held aloft in just one hand, Sir Mortimer urged the warhorse down the aisle towards the Abbot and Sister Cecelia and just for a moment I could have sworn that the huge, wild-eyed stallion snorted fire from his nostrils. Pulling his dripping cock from Sister Cecelia's juicing, clasping cunt, the Abbot pushed her into the arms of the Prioress, trying to find a means of escape. But there was none.

Reining his mount to a scrambling halt, the knight levelled his sword to the Abbot's throat, forcing him back up against the altar. A terrible heart-stopping roar arose from behind his visor, filling all present with dread before he called upon God for help as with a voice of thunder he chanted a ritual invocation.

"Demon spawn of the Devil, I order you back from whence you came; back to the fires of Hades, back to Lucifer your master. Back I say, be gone and take your satanic followers with you."

Even now, all these years later I still cannot believe what I saw next. Letting out a hideous shriek, the Abbot seemed to shrink inside his cassock, putrefied flesh peeling from his face and body until just a skull and bare bones remained. And these too did not remain for long, crumbling into dust before the horrified eyes of the Sisters; for apart from me they were now alone, every single one of the congregation of monks having suffered the same fate as the Abbot.

Raising his visor, Sir Mortimer's piercing gaze fell upon the Prioress and his ravaged, naked daughter. But his words were not what I expected to hear. The rescue of Sister Cecelia had been the last thing on his mind and thinking back I realise that I should not have been surprised, for he had sent her to the convent precisely for the purpose of servicing the Abbot and the monks.

"Mother Superior, I beg your forgiveness for my desecration of your chapel, but it could not be helped. My fellow knights have brought to my ears disturbing tales of weary travellers being offered rest and succour in the monastery only to be set upon, robbed and subjected to all manner of hideous sexual perversions before being murdered by the monks.

"So I came to find out the truth and in the monastery I discovered the true extent of their evil. I found the black altar and all the paraphernalia of devil worship that these evil beings used in their glorification of Satan. I could not allow them to carry on with their foul doings and by my vows as a Christian knight, it was my duty to send them to hell where they belong. This I have done.

"No blame lies with you and your nuns for I truly believe that you had no knowledge of what was happening so close to you. You may carry on in peace with no fear of interference from me."

Sister Cecelia had been sheltering in the arms of the Prioress and it was she whom he addressed next.

"Cecelia, you are no longer a daughter of mine but a daughter of the church. However now that I see you naked, abused and distraught, with the Abbot's sperm dripping from your box, I offer you a choice. If you so wish you may return with me to the shelter of the castle, or you may remain here. I offer you this choice once only, so decide wisely."

The Prioress held her close, lightly stroking her breasts and one hand slipping between her thighs to caress her leaking love hole as Sister Cecelia made her reply.

"I thank you my father for allowing me to determine

my own future. I am content here with the Prioress and my sister nuns and by your grace I will stay with them."

"So be it. Now I depart and possibly may never set eyes on you again. Live long and be happy."

And then, it was to me that his attention was attracted. I was no longer needed in the convent, he told the Prioress and he was therefore returning me to his own household. Joy overwhelmed me. I was to be set free once again to enjoy the magnificence of knightly life and I was not sorry to be leaving, although I did feel a small pang of sadness at parting from Sister Cecelia.

As we left the chapel I saw that she appeared to be suffering no such sorrows, for she was passionately embracing the Prioress, her tongue eagerly searching for the Prioress' own and her hands squeezing and fondling her ample breasts.

Yes, I thought, Sister Cecelia will be happy here.

As we thundered out through the chapel doors, and I have never known why, I felt a great compulsion to take one last look back into the haven of contentment that I had enjoyed while being responsible for Sister Cecelia's discipline and continuing submissive behaviour. And for the second time that fateful night, I was shocked to the core. The chapel was alive with the wailing of tortured souls; banshee wails that were shrieking from the mouths of the sisters. Sisters who were now swooping through the chapel on flapping leathery wings.

And the shrieks were awful blood-curdling screams that I had last experienced one hundred or more years earlier when I had been in the service of Sir Mortimer's grandfather and along with him had been included on a mission to free the Holy Land from the Muslim hordes. It is said by those who falsely claim to know, that the Knights Templar found the Holy Grail hidden away in a secret chamber beneath the temple in Jerusalem; but I know that that is not so, for I had seen then the same awful thing that I was seeing at that moment - hideous, blood sucking apparitions from Hell.

Vampires!

Monstrous creations of Satan with whom The Brotherhood had been in constant battle since time immemorial, until in one final night of slaughter they believed that they had finally rid the Earth of the foul creatures. But they had been wrong. It was not only a secret chamber that lay beneath the temple but connected to it were a series of catacombs, and in those dark, dank surroundings the Templars discovered a nest of surviving blood drinkers. And it was the task of destroying those vile creatures of the night that kept the knights occupied for so long. They did nothing to dispel the rumours that they had discovered the Holy Grail as it kept the inquisitive from probing too deeply into their affairs. No one must be allowed to find out that vampires were loose in the Lord's Holy city and so they let it be known that keeping the Grail safe was their Holy responsibility. Anyone trying to find their way into the chamber was threatened with death. After a few summary executions, the lesson was well learnt and very few ever again tried to do so.

One by one, the evil monsters were hunted down and executed by plunging a stake through its heart until once again they believed that none of them remained. Christians could once more sleep soundly in their beds.

But now it seemed as if that were not so, for there they were, before my very eyes!

And worst of all, as Sir Mortimer urged his steed onwards, I saw the Prioress lift her head away from Sister Cecelia's searching mouth. Her lips curled back and two razor-sharp fangs dug deep into Sister Cecelia's neck; her jugular spurting a fountain of the scarlet elixir of life. But what could I do? I am mute, incapable of speech and so I was carried away back the castle by an unknowing Sir Mortimer. A Sir Mortimer who apart from his many other duties, was pledged to fight and destroy those evil, blood sucking, soul-gathering creatures of the night that now had enslaved his daughter and consigned her to an infinity of wretchedness. Like them, she would ever onwards have to dedicate her life, not to the glory of God, but to the never-ending quest for fresh human blood.

Falconer is a unique talent who delights in taking the genre into new territory every time he writes. He is also one of the very few writers; Francine Whittaker being the only other who springs to mind, who can successfully write male dom and fem dom.

His male dom titles are:

    Tales from the Lodge (with Sean O'Kane)

    The Brotherhood

    The Pit of Pain.

His fem dom titles are:

    The Daughters of de Sade

    Slaves of the Bloodline.

"Last Resort"

or "Ypiog"

by William Avon

William is an immensely talented artist and writer. His illustrations for Slaveworld and Royal Slave are familiar to members of the readers' club. Here he offers a pungent and sharp little tale.

They kept Lesley in a box of thick marine-ply sheets, bolted solidly together. It had a single door at one end with a small viewing slot cut into it, which was covered by an external hinged flap like a letterbox. When this was closed the box became a cramped prison cell, which would have been totally dark except for the light filtering through the rows of small vent holes drilled in its sides. It was too low for her to sit up in, and only just long enough to stretch out full length. The floor was padded with a foam rubber matt and a single pillow. She was kept naked at all times, of course, and there were no sheets, but as the cell room was warm that was the least of her worries.

While in the cell box her wrists were manacled together and the middle of the chain was clipped to a large ring mounted on the broad black leather collar buckled about her neck. A metal tag hung from the ring like a dog tag. On it was stamped: "BITCH 3"

Had she been able to use her fingers she could have unclipped the chain and unbuckled her collar. But her fingers were enclosed in thumbless, mitten-like padded gloves of black rubber that were themselves buckled firmly about her wrists. Nothing she would be required to do while in captivity required any dexterity on her part, while the effective loss of her fingers only added to her helplessness and shame.

Normally she could never have slept under such conditions, but by the end of each day she was so exhausted she fell asleep almost before the cell door was closed behind her. It was only the rattle of the padlock being unfastened the next morning that roused her to another day of torment...

'Get your sorry ass out here, Number 3!' a man snapped in deep, commanding tones.

It was Mike Last. Lesley trembled at the sound of his voice and hastened to obey.

She had to crawl backwards out of her cell. As soon as her head emerged Last grasped her collar and clipped a chain to the ring. He was a lean, strong man, with coffee-dark skin flowing over rippling muscles; his perfectly toned body barely concealed by tight singlet and shorts. Taking hold of the other end of the leash he walked her along at his heel like a dog.

Moving on hands and knees with the manacles in place meant Lesley had to shuffle forward with her nose almost touching the ground, her full breasts rubbing over the boards, tormenting her treacherously erect nipples, and her bare bottom wiggling in the air so that her deep-cleft pubic pouch was blatantly exposed. None of this, she was sure, was unintentional. The stinging slaps Last delivered with a rubber-bladed paddle across her invitingly upraised buttocks as she went were certainly deliberate. She gasped as each blow landed but said nothing, knowing her captors never left marks that would show later.

She shuffled past a row of cell-boxes identical to hers. At least three were occupied at this moment, but of course she would never know the names of the women inside them or even see their faces. Occasionally she heard them responding to their keepers or else moaning and yelping in pain as they were punished, but they were referred to only by their numbers. Their actual names were never mentioned in the hearing of their sister prisoners. Like her, all that happened here would remain a dark secret bound by shame.

Next to the cell-room was a bathroom fitted with a Turkish-style toilet. Lesley shuffled round and squatted over it. Keeping her legs wide and eyes lowered she voided her wastes. When she was done, Last made a note of the quantity she had excreted then pressed a plunger button on the wall. Water jets washed her groin clean.

Still dripping, Lesley was led into the next room. It was a large chamber partitioned into a number of cubicles, each containing its particular torment.

In the first cubicle a plate of food was already set out on the floor. She had to eat it like a dog, without using either cutlery or fingers. Chopped fruit and whole grains mixed with a little sunflower oil, which bound it into soft lumps. It was highly nutritious but lacked bulk, so that she felt hungry even after she had dutifully licked the plate clean.

Given little time to digest her spartan meal, she was then put on the treadmill.

Lesley's glistening breasts bounced as she pounded the endless track. The sweat dripped onto the rubber belt under her feet, making it slippery. But she dare not fall, nor could she even rest.

The sides of the treadmill had been filled with sloping perspex panels, so it was impossible to step off onto the tread boards that flanked the belt. She could not run forward or back off the belt because of the restraining plug up her rear.

It was a mushroom-headed prong of rubber, mounted on the end of a metal arm that extended from a stand behind the treadmill. The arm was pivoted and had a sprung telescoping middle section, which meant it followed the motion of her body as she ran and did not impede her stride. But this was a strictly limited degree of freedom.

Sensors in the arm measured the compression of its joints. If Lesley slowed down a control box would send electric shocks of increasing intensity along wires taped to the arm which terminated in crocodile clips clamped to her labia; clips that with her gloved hands, of course, she could not release.

The warning shocks were both painful and perversely stimulating to her vulva, so that after a while she was not sure if they were a punishment or a reward. She pounded on in a confused haze of misery and excitement with hard nipples and erect clitoris, while humiliating lubrication trickled down the insides of her thighs to join the sweat staining the track.

Midday was always testing time. Lesley's heart thudded as she was led through the door of the testing cubicle.

Jasmine Last was always present for testing. She was dressed like Mike and her body was equally well toned.

Her erect nipples crowned the firm rounded swells of her breasts like thimbles. Holstered in a belt slung about her slim waist were not only a rubber-bladed paddle but also an electric cattle prod. Beside her was a high-backed wooden frame chair fitted with an ominous array of straps.

Together the couple removed Lesley's manacles and sat her down in the chair. She struggled feebly as they were strapping her in. This was merely a reflex response and quite pointless as they were too strong to resist. A light slap across the cheek from Jasmine drove the flicker of resistance from her. When the spring-toothed jaws of crocodile clips trailing electric wires closed about her nipples she gave only a stifled gasp of pain.

When she was secure they stepped back, looking her over with expert, slightly contemptuous eyes.

Broad rubber straps crossed her chest between her heavy trembling breasts, dug into the soft swell of her stomach, secured her wrists to the tops of the armrests and encircled her knees and ankles; dragging her thighs wide so they could see her plump, golden-fleeced pubic cleft. The chair had no proper seat, just narrow padded boards forming a "V" under her widespread legs. Beneath her exposed, fleshy buttocks was a plastic bucket.

Under her captors' gaze Lesley trembled, both from shame and guilt. It was all her fault that she was here. How could she have been so weak-minded? And now she was going to be made to suffer for it...

'Now, let's see what a miserable specimen you really are,' Mike said. He pressed a button marked: "TEST", which was mounted on a box of electronics connected to the stand on which the chair rested.

The box beeped angrily, a red light flashed and a synthesised voice shouted: 'Fail! Fail! Fail...'

With each damning word a jolt of electricity stabbed into Lesley's clamped nipples. She shrieked and writhed in her bonds.

The pain was such that she lost control of herself and fitful spurts of urine were driven out of her into the waiting bucket.

After what seemed like an eternity, though it could not in fact have been more than ten seconds, the jolts ceased. Lesley hung her head, sobbing in her bonds, her blonde mane tumbling over her bare shoulders. But Mike grasped a fistful of hair and jerked her head up so that she looked into his eyes.

'You're a stupid, fat, white bitch!' he said. 'What are you...?'

'I'm... a stupid... fat... white bitch...' Lesley mumbled back.

'And what are we going to do to you?' he asked.

'What... whatever you have to,' Lesley whispered.

'Even if it hurts?' Jasmine asked, a malicious grin on her pretty face.

'I... deserve to be hurt. I've got to suffer... to learn not to be so stupid again...' As always Lesley felt dizzy with wonder at her own words. It was perversely good to confess her sin aloud, even though she knew what it would mean.

They freed her from the chair and threw her back down onto her hands and knees. As Jasmine knelt before her and took hold of her collar, Mike stripped off his shorts, releasing his swelling manhood.

Kicking Lesley's ankles wider he knelt between her shins.

As he took hold of her hips, she felt the velvety head of his cock brush across the cleft of her buttocks as it sought the mouth of her vagina.

He forced his thick shaft into Lesley until it was buried to the hilt, driving a gasp of pain from her lungs as she was stretched wide. Jasmine stroked her cheek and smiled at her discomfort. Lesley knew this act of disciplining would leave bruises, but not where they would show.

As Mike began to pump her hot wet depths, he bent forward and growled in her ear: 'What would your friends say if they could see you now?'

Lesley sobbed in shame even as she felt herself helplessly responding to his cruel thrusts. Her friends would not believe it, of course. But they would never know...

He clasped her swaying breasts, kneading their hot fleshy fullness, then pinched and twisted her nipples.

'Whose fault is it you're here?'

'Mine!' Lesley whimpered. 'It's all mine...'

'And will you do what you're told and work hard?"

'Yes, yes!'

She orgasmed even before he came inside her; which was both a blissful release and deeply shaming. While she was still sprawled on the floor, Mike pulled his glistening cock out of her, wiped it dry on a handful of her hair, then jerked her head up.

'What do you say?'

'Thank you...' she mumbled. 'Thank you...'

On some afternoons she was put in the sunroom to continue tanning her too-pale flesh to a more acceptable tone. However the process was nothing so restful as lying on a simple sun bed. She had to work while she tanned.

Her mittens were removed so that she was totally naked apart from protective goggles. Transparent plastic straps were used to secure her wrists and ankles to cables running through tension reels. These dragged her into a standing spread-eagled posture in the middle of the circular room, which was ringed by UV tubes. A plastic rod coiled about with bare copper wire and trailing an electric flex was slid up her rectum. The rod was too thin for her muscles to expel. Its flex was connected to another electronic control box.

As soon as the tanning lights came on she had to began making star jumps, working against the tension on the cables, or else receive a sharp anal shock that made her buttocks clench convulsively. The motion set her breasts bouncing even more vigorously than on the treadmill. She came out of the sunroom dripping with sweat and aching in every limb.

Gradually the days blurred into an endless round of running and stretching and straining against springs, punctuated by the dread verdict of the testing chair and the shame of what followed. There was some variety. On a couple of occasions the Lasts set her working with another of their captives, though of course Lesley never knew who...

Gagged and blindfolded, Lesley sat opposite the other woman, whose legs like hers were splayed wide, their ankles chained to rings set in the floor. Between them was an upright lever with a "T" bar top to which their wrists were chained. If they worked together leaning forward and then back, the lever could be rocked against the resistance of heavy springs.

For once pain was used only to start them off; the ongoing incentive was degrading pleasure. The lever was connected at its base to two horizontal rods that extended out to the apex of their spread legs. These rods were capped by soft rubber dildos, which had been partially inserted into their gaping vulvas. Each time Lesley pushed the lever forward her dildo was thrust all the way up her.

Lesley and her unseen partner had by now reached such a desperate and shameless state of mind that they gladly cooperated in this act of mutual mechanical masturbation, exhausting as it was, to save them from more conventional punishment. They remained coupled together for five hours, during which Lesley orgasmed three times and she suspected her sister sufferer went one better.

On alternate days, after Lesley had failed the testing chair, Jasmine laid her on her back along a narrow bench and strapped her firmly down. Then she shed her own shorts and sat astride Lesley's head so that she could look down the length of her tightly bound body.

'I want to feel your tongue in me, bitch!' she commanded, grinding her slippery, spicy scented pudenda with its tight dark curls into Lesley's upturned face.

Helplessly, Lesley obeyed, licking out the intricate folds of flesh that enveloped nose and mouth. If she was pleasing, Jasmine contented herself with kneading Lesley's softly mounded breasts and tweaking her engorged nipples playfully. If she was not satisfied, Jasmine slid the tip of her electric goad into Lesley's by now dripping vagina and encouraged her to greater efforts with shocks of increasing intensity.

Jasmine did not rise from her living pleasure seat until she came, when she drenched Lesley's face with her juices.

Every night Lesley fell asleep thinking of the shame of it all. The terrible, wonderful shame...

Then came the day when the testing chair controller flashed green. Instead of "Fail" it said: 'Passed, passed!'

Lesley, dazed and confused, was still braced for the pain. But no shock came.

'Sixty grammes under your target weight,' Mike Last pronounced with satisfaction. 'Number 3; you will wear that holiday bikini!'

Half an hour later, Lesley, now properly dressed, was pressing a cheque into Mike's hand and babbling blushing thanks. Jasmine showed her out and closed the outer door behind her. Outside the door was a discreet brass plate that read:

Last Resort Bodyshaping

M & J Last

YPIOG

Another satisfied customer had departed; her guilt over a little excess fat purged by suffering and humiliation, perhaps even secretly proud at what she had endured. Now she was eager to show off her newly trim, pre-holiday tanned body to her friends, after her fortnight away visiting that obscure relative she had never mentioned before. Maybe Lesley would be back, maybe she wouldn't, but Mike and Jasmine knew there would be more like her; women with more money than willpower, who felt they had to get in shape whatever it cost.

Curiously, none of them ever asked what the cryptic initials on the plate stood for.

Your Pain Is Our Gain.

William has contributed two brilliantly conceived and plotted alternative reality novels to the Silver Moon catalogue;

The Girlspell

Slaves of the Girlspell

He is also a highly talented artist and if you want to see his illustrative work, contact the readers' club – details at the end of the book.

DARK SURRENDER

BY KIM KNIGHT

Leigh Goldman, a young psychotherapist is disturbed and strangely fascinated by Mel, a young girl who calmly relates to her, her experiences of harsh sexual dominance at the hands of her master. Leigh has never come across the world of SM and is soon out of her depth as she desperately tries to help Mel escape from her slavery.

First she must find who the strange and sinister master is, then she must convince him that she is a dominant too. But most importantly she has to explore her own sexuality to the very limits and that leads her into darker and stranger places than she could ever have imagined.

Kim Knight makes an impressive debut in Dark Surrender. It is intended as the first of a series of self-contained novels under the collective title; 'Unchained'.

Puritan Punishment

By Caroline Swift

London under Oliver Cromwell was not the haven of temperate sobriety history has led us to believe!

These diaries, kept by a young maid who was left in the care of her drunken aunt and uncle, reveal a hotbed of lust and depravity. As Janet, cast out by her relatives for refusing to submit to their desires, soon discovers, London is a dangerous place for a pretty ingénue.

Refuge under the roof of the dominant Lady Postell comes at a high price, but it is one Janet finds she is willing to pay. Journeying to Maveringham and Winscombe Abbey she encounters a host of dominant lovers but foolishly is persuaded into attempting to escape. This is a dangerous course of action when recapture could expose her to the full force of Puritan Punishment!

This is Caroline Swift at her erotic, graphic and eloquent best.

Parisian Punishment

By Caroline Swift

A young English girl arrives in 17th. century France as the property of the dominant Francine de Clavaux and her handsome husband Gilles. She is cast headlong into the licentious affairs of the French nobility and the brothels of Paris. Dominant lover follows dominant lover as Janet's owners take her through the treachery and the bedrooms of the turbulent times, until finally she and the lovely Larissa fins themselves back in the England of Cromwell. But even there all is not plain sailing.

There are very few writers who can match Caroline Swift's knowing and highly charged evocations of castles and dungeons; slaves and their masters and mistresses.

A Slave's Desire

By Kim Knight

Mel, recently freed from slavery, is determined to win her lover's freedom. But Natalie is still a slave and has been sold into slavery in Russia. Helped by the mysterious Claudia, Mel tracks her but is foiled at the last minute.

The vicious mistress' called 'Faith' has had the beautiful Natalie taken to a training camp in Algeria. Here her torment seems never-ending and she sinks into complete submission.

Inventive, cruel and clever; Kim Knight's second volume in the 'Unchained' series is as absorbing as it is highly erotic.

The Chains That Bind

By Kim Knight

Claudia is trying to shake off the attraction she still feels for the dangerous dominatrix, Mistress Faith. But she is hampered by her feelings for the two submissives she shares a flat with, Natalie and Mel. Claudia is torn between her desire to free herself from a past that still torments her and her desire for Faith.

But there is also the sinister Kelso to contend with. He is determined that if she re-enters the SM world, it will be as his slave.

'The Chains that Bind' is the third in Kim Knight's brilliant 'Unchained' series of stand-alone novels. She brings an originality to erotica centred on female sexuality which is uniquely hers - and the action just goes on getting hotter!

Slave House

By Kim Knight

"They left her black thong on and Leigh stepped forward to stroke her smooth buttock with the palm of her hand. She turned to Greg who was watching her with wide, lust-filled eyes.

'Very nice,' Leigh commented as she ran her hand down the back of her thighs. 'What do you two think?'

Alicia and Star studied the hanging submissive and then looked at each other before Star replied, 'She's pretty.'

'She needs a woman's touch,' Leigh announced."

Leigh Goldman is reluctantly drawn back into the shadowy world of SM at the request of an old friend, the beautiful submissive Mel. Together they enter the sinister Slave House to try and rescue another slave. Kim Knight's inventive and knowledgeable take on sex and SM makes for more unmissabloe reading as the tangled lines of dominance and submission become almost as intricately knotted as the bondage that imprisons the beautiful slaves.

The Roman Slavegirl

By Syra Bond

'Magnus smacked her hard, each time bringing his hand down more firmly. The loud smacks caused Bec to tense her body until it was rigid, but she did not cry out, nor did she squirm or try to avoid the blows. Caristia looked at Bec's taut body and listened to the regular rhythm of Magnus's smacking hand. She leant back against the wall — almost hidden by the shadows — and allowed her hand to drift……'

A beautiful, flaxen haired Saxon girl, captured and enslaved, is bound to cause a stir in Pompeii. And once she arrives at the house of Rufo the slave dealer and comes under the discipline of Magnus, his trainer, Caristia has no choice but to experience every aspect of their brutal world; a world that demands complete submission from her.

Into the Arena

By Sean O'Kane

Tara is a thrill seeker; a girl who pits herself against as many challenges as she can. But when she meets Conor Brien she finds herself facing greater tests than she could ever have imagined.

He is scouting for female gladiators to take part in the recreated Roman games he and his associates are planning to stage - and he wants Tara.

But before they are ready, these modern gladiators have to learn to please their owners and the crowds who will throng the stands and cheer them on as they battle against each other on the sands of the arenas.

On board a ship which transports them towards their new life, Tara and her companions are faced with stark choices. Will they submit to the harsh training regime which is imposed upon them? Will they march out to do battle for their owner?

The Gladiator

By Sean O'Kane

With her training now behind her, Tara is ready for the arena. She throws herself eagerly into all the contests her maser enters her for and soon becomes a star performer. But there are others in the stable she fights for who have different agendas. Unwittingly she becomes the focus of jealousy and a bitter power struggle.

And while the masters fight over her, Tara herself must endure whatever the arenas can throw at her.

In this, the second of Sean O'Kane's 'Arena' series, he tells a gripping tale of sex and intrigue while all the time the beautiful gladiators battle it out on the arena sands.

Slave's Honour

By Sean O'Kane

The modern arenas go from strength to strength! The spectacles are becoming more and more magnificent – and more and more slaves are required.

Brian Holden has just secured the job every young man wants; deputy to the master slave trainer Carlo Suarez. Blondie, El Tigre and Jet are just some of his beautiful charges and as he learns the secrets of his craft he also learns about the treacherous web of power politics that surround him. When the beautiful new groom arrives to help with the gladiators and pony girls, he finds that nowhere is safe from the quarrels between the Owners.

This is the fourth in the acclaimed Arena series and while the gorgeous gladiators like Ayesha and the slave known only as 'Snake' provide entertainment for the crowds out on the sands of the arena floors, their masters continue to manipulate their property.

Atmospheric and darkly erotic, Slave's Honour continues to develop Sean's seductive cast of characters against a background of deliciously cruel entertainment.

Tales from the Lodge

By Sean O'Kane and Falconer Bridges

For the first time ever Silver Moon readers can get a glimpse into the world of the super rich SM devotees.

From Brittany comes Oliver's account of how the lovely Marie-Helene introduced him to the delights of mastery.

From the gorgeous Lolli comes a story of schoolgirl passion which resulted in a devastating sexual awakening.

Caroline recalls how her husband John started The Lodge and how she came to be one of its first servants after training by both him and Madame Stalevsky.

Taming the Brat

By Sean O'Kane

When Alan Masterson, a successful businessman, is challenged to control and tame Laura Andreotti, a tempestuous American heiress, two very strong willed people are thrown together, but who will prove the stronger? And who will tame who?

Played out against the background of an SM world that only the very rich can afford, the contest of wills between the beautiful but spoilt Laura and the dominant Alan brings two of the most unforgettable characters in the Silver Moon catalogue vividly to life. And their struggle is one of the most erotic you'll ever read.

Last Slave Standing

By Sean O'Kane

"'Your master, your real master, Raika is a man of his word. Just do a little job for him and he will make sure you are looked after....' Sir John's voice was soft and seductive but she couldn't betray her home; not even for the promise of a return to her birthplace and a life of respectability. Wordlessly she shook her head and braced herself for the retribution that would surely follow her refusal.

But none came.

Instead she felt his hand on her arm and he was leading her across to the windowless dungeon that occupied the whole of one end of the stable block."

Raika is faced with an impossible choice. Which master is she supposed to serve; the one who owns her now or the one who sold her to him for a very specific and sinister purpose? And whichever way she chooses she will be in great danger, and so will others.

In a story crowded with intensely erotic images of pony slaves and their grooms, masters and trainers, Sean O'Kane's vision of the world of the arenas and their competing squads of slaves reaches new heights of ingenuity culminating in the ultimate challenge of the game they call 'Last Slave Standing'

Sweet Submissions Vol I

Various Authors

'Rachel listened to a distant clock strike noon and knew her ordeal had begun. Nervousness tightened her chest. She took a deep breath around the ball-gag, tested the cuffs that held her wrists above her head, and told herself there was now no chance to go back.'

Rachel submits to some harsh trials at the hands of a range of masters. But hers is only one in a devastatingly erotic series of Sweet Submissions.

Isabella Vanelli, stunningly beautiful and talented finds out that in the hands of a master, her body rules her head. Giselle Lorimer is at her absolute best.

Annabel, Melissa and Paula all find that there is nothing they won't do for their master; 'The Patriarch'. Sean O'Kane revisits the 'Church of Chains'.

Emma finds an English city is rife with those dedicated to SM and must decide whether she will submit or not. And if she does, there is a high price to pay. Emma Stewart writes straight from the heart.

Joan's master catches her out behaving in a manner way above her station in life and makes her pay for it. Kim Knight's intense and dark explorations of female submission continue.

On one wild night, Norma Jean is put through her paces by Joe in ways she had never imagined possible. Falconer Bridges brings his unique talents to bear on a beautiful submissive.

Six unforgettable submissions from some of Silver Moon's top talent!

Sil Mo

The Best in

Return to Eden
Stephen Rawlings

Silvana's Guest
Caroline Swift

Controlling Catherine
Elena Gregory

A Slave's Desire
Kim Knight

Enslaving Anna
Giselle Lorimer

221

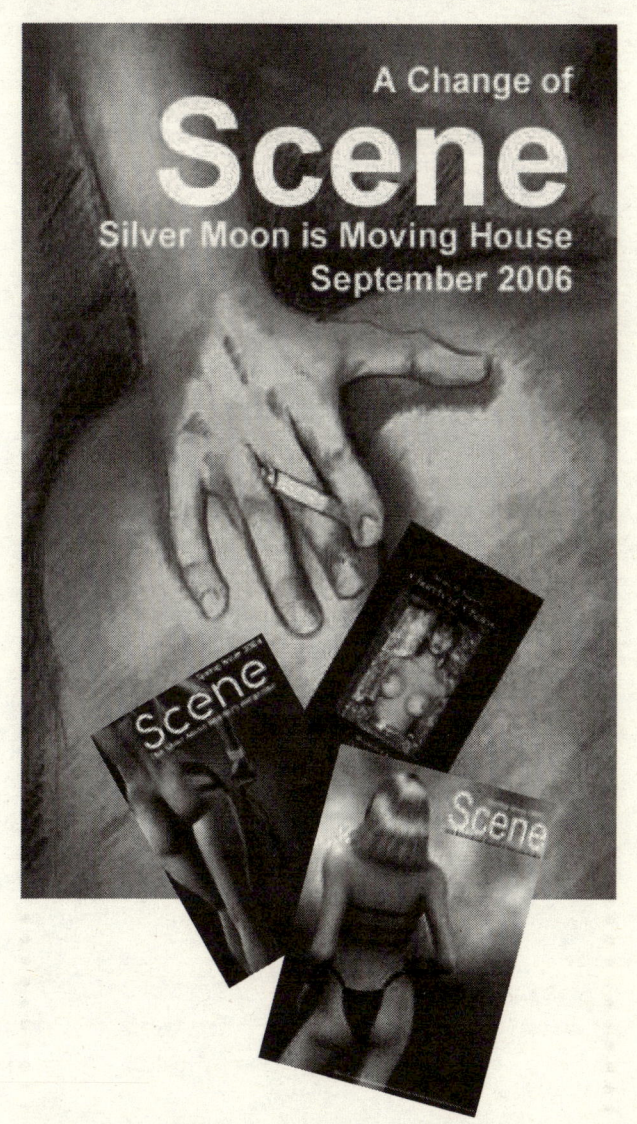

Scene, the Silver Moon Readers' Club magazine is sent free of charge to all UK members.

There are over 100 stunningly erotic novels of domination and submission in the Silver Moon catalogue. You can see the full range, including Club and Illustrated editions by writing to:

Silver Moon Reader Services
Shadowline Publishing Ltd,
No 2 Granary Road,
Gainsborough,
Lincs. DH21 2NS

You will receive a copy of the latest issue of the Readers' Club magazine, with articles, features, reviews, adverts and news plus a full list of our publications and an order form.